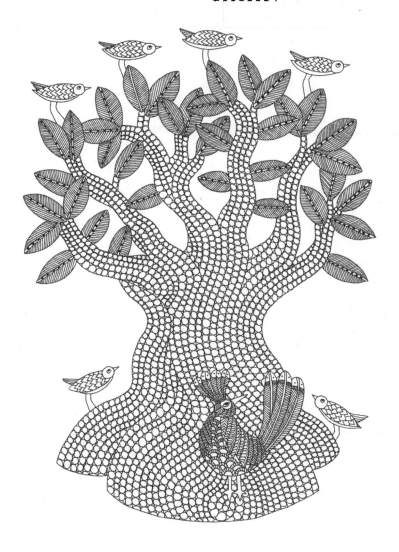

PUFFIN BOOKS

the wishbird

the wishbird

GABRIELLE WANG

Illustrations by the author

PUFFIN BOOKS

PUFFIN BOOKS

Published by the Penguin Group
Penguin Group (Australia)
707 Collins Street, Melbourne, Victoria 3008, Australia
(a division of Pearson Australia Group Pty Ltd)
Penguin Group (USA) Inc.
375 Hudson Street, New York, New York 10014, USA
Penguin Group (Canada)
90 Eglinton Avenue East, Suite 700, Toronto, Canada ON M4P 2Y3
(a division of Pearson Penguin Canada Inc.)
Penguin Books Ltd
80 Strand, London WC2R 0RL England
Penguin Ireland
25 St Stephen's Green, Dublin 2, Ireland
(a division of Penguin Books Ltd)
Penguin Books India Pvt Ltd
11 Community Centre, Panchsheel Park, New Delhi – 110 017, India
Penguin Group (NZ)
67 Apollo Drive, Rosedale, Auckland 0632, New Zealand
(a division of Pearson New Zealand Ltd)
Penguin Books (South Africa) (Pty) Ltd
Rosebank Office Park, Block D,
181 Jan Smuts Avenue, Parktown North, Johannesburg, 2196, South Africa
Penguin (Beijing) Ltd
7F, Tower B, Jiaming Center, 27 East Third Ring Road North,
Chaoyang District, Beijing 100020, China

Penguin Books Ltd, Registered Offices: 80 Strand, London, WC2R 0RL, England

First published by Penguin Group (Australia), 2013

1 3 5 7 9 10 8 6 4 2

Text and illustrations copyright © Gabrielle Wang, 2013.

The moral right of the author/illustrator has been asserted.

Cover and text design by Tony Palmer © Penguin Group (Australia)
Illustrations by Gabrielle Wang
Cover illustration background © Nella/Shutterstock
Cover title script © Danny Rash/Shutterstock
Colour separation by Splitting Image Colour Studio, Clayton, Victoria
Printed and bound in Australia by McPherson's Printing Group, Maryborough, Victoria

National Library of Australia Cataloguing-in-Publication data:

ISBN 978 0 14 330752 5

puffin.com.au

For Mum with love

PROLOGUE

In the ancient Banyan tree, the Wishbird lay still and silent. His breath was thin, the thread between the King and himself growing ever weaker. Soon it would break, and when that time came, both would die, and so would the city, for its heart would be lost forever.

But death did not worry the Wishbird. He had lived for a thousand years and more. And he would go on living, in another shape, another form – in the clouds, in the earth, in the lakes and seas.

What did worry him was Oriole. Sweet Oriole.

1
LITTLE THIEF

On the edge of the Borderlands, in the City of Soulless, a small figure crouched in the shadow of the old wooden drum tower.

His name was Boy, a name given to him by Panther who had plucked him off the streets. Being an orphan he had no idea how many years old he was. Somewhere between eight and ten winters, Rabbit had told him.

Boy stood suddenly and, slipping from shadow into light, fell into step behind an elderly man. The man wore a hat with the brim low over his face, but it didn't quite hide the hook-shaped scar down his left cheek. He stopped to buy a stick of candied cumquats, then paid the vendor and placed his drawstring purse back inside his sleeve.

Now. Boy bumped the man as if by accident. At the same moment, his hand glided inside his wide sleeve and withdrew the purse with a touch as light as air.

'Excuse me, Uncle,' he said politely, slipping the purse into his pocket and melting away into the crowd.

Panther won't cane me this time, he thought, feeling the pleasing weight of the coins against his leg and wincing as the large red welts on his back twinged. Boy knew he should return to the shack where Panther would be waiting. But what if there was something else inside the purse – a small treasure that he could keep for himself?

Every so often he found strange and beautiful objects when he light-fingered people's pockets. The head of a cat made from glowing amber. A silver ring with a tiny blue stone like a mouse's tear. And once a piece of red cloth edged in the finest gold thread. He had fifteen of these treasures buried in a box in the dirt beneath his bedding.

So Boy walked past the well where women were washing clothes, under the archway that led into the market square, and along Palace Road. Finally he turned down Burnt Water Lane.

At the sound of his footfall, a rat as big as a soldier's boot scurried along a shallow ditch of putrid water. Boy glanced around, then slipped into a narrow passageway between two wooden buildings.

With his back against one wall and his belly against the other, he sidled along until he reached a spot where several large foundation stones had fallen away, forming a little cave. Boy crawled inside and sat down cross-legged. Then he tipped the contents of the purse into his lap.

Suddenly he grew very still. His breath caught in his throat as if someone had punched the air right out of him.

There amongst the coins was a small, thin silver box. The lid was attached by two tiny hinges and at the front was a gleaming pearl clasp. He carefully snapped it open.

Even more beautiful than the box was the object inside it. The thing fitted perfectly into its container and was a brilliant turquoise blue. He lifted it out carefully. On either side of the almost transparent shaft were soft filaments that separated at his touch then returned to their original shape.

As Boy turned it slowly in his fingers a strange thing began to happen. A face appeared, drifting up from his memories. It was only faint, as though Boy was looking through the finest rice paper, but there it was – smiling eyes, soft, rose-coloured lips, gleaming black hair and a jade-coloured earring. His heartbeat quickened.

Panther often told Boy the story of how he had found him on the streets, dirty and starving, and in the goodness of his heart had taken him in. But one day Rabbit, Panther's friend, had shown him a house in a little laneway in a forgotten part of the city, and told him a different story.

He told of how Panther had heard that yet another family had been taken away. It was good news. It meant an empty house and easy pickings: food and belongings left behind as if the family had rushed off and would soon return. But those who had been taken never returned.

Panther and Rabbit had hurried to the house before the news spread. But when they were gathering the belongings they heard crying. It was Rabbit who found the small boy hidden in a trunk in one of the bedrooms and convinced Panther to take him in, convinced him how useful he would be when he was old enough to light-finger.

Boy's memories had always been like a constantly shifting mirage, a pebble dropped into a pond where the waters had grown muddy. Now, as he stared at this beautiful object in his hand, the memories gradually grew clearer.

For the first time he felt hope that his mother and father might still be alive.

'Your ata was called Master Rui,' Rabbit had told Boy the first time he showed him the house where he had been found. 'And your ana, she was Madame Naa.'

'What happened to them?' Boy had asked. 'Why did they leave me behind?'

'Soldiers came an' took them away in the Song Stealer's Cart,' Rabbit had replied.

'What did they do wrong?'

'I dunno. But we thought you was dumb or something 'cos you didn't make a noise for weeks. Just sat in the corner like a scared little mouse.' Rabbit had laid his hands on Boy's shoulders. 'You mustn't tell Panther I brung you here. Swear in the name of the God of Honourable

Thieves that you won't tell Panther or he'll punish me.'

Boy had taken the oath and kept the secret close to his heart. But he often visited the house and stared up at its grand façade where weeds sprouted through the tiled roof like the bushy eyebrows of an old man.

Once, with the edge of his sleeve, he had wiped the dirt off a small bronze plaque attached to the wall by the front door. Slowly, three characters had emerged. Boy had never learned to read or write so he asked Rabbit what they said.

'*Golden Note Studio,*' Rabbit had replied.

'What does that mean?' Boy asked.

Rabbit had shrugged.

Those few strange words were all that were left of his parents.

A wind blew down the narrow passageway like an angry dragon lashing out with its tail, and Boy suddenly realised that the sun had dipped below the city wall, leaving the small alcove where he'd been sitting cold and dark. He had stayed too long.

Panther will be furious. But at least I have a purse full of money. That should keep him happy . . . for a while anyway.

He slipped the silver box with its precious treasure inside one of the many pockets deep in his sleeve and hurried back to the shack at the bottom of Ratskin Alley.

2
THE CRYING TREE

While the wind whistled through the streets of the City of Soulless, far far away in a moonlit forest a huge nest swayed gently in the branches of an ancient Banyan tree.

The nest was made from fragrant Sandalwood twigs and lined with soft moss. And there, curled up under a cloak of rainbow feathers, a girl lay sleeping.

Ooop Ooop Ooop

A Hoopoe bird with a magnificent crest of golden feathers landed on a nearby branch.

Oriole opened her eyes. They were the colour of emeralds with small flecks of brown. She sat up and flicked back her long, dark hair. At the corners of her lips there was a whisper of a smile as if she was about to share a secret.

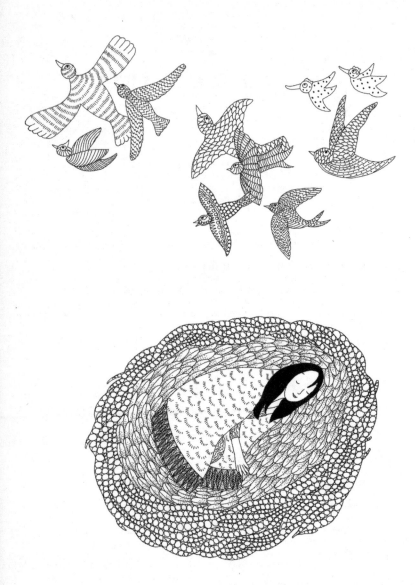

'Good morning, Mellow,' Oriole said in a melodic voice. She rubbed her eyes and stretched, then touched the bird on its cheek. 'Are you feeling well? You look tired.'

Mellow sighed. 'Purplewing swallowed a pebble which he mistook for a seed. And Redbill and Droplet were fighting again, this time for the best position at Fern Pond.'

Oriole laughed. 'Everything looks like food to Purplewing. And Redbill and Droplet are quarrelsome by nature. They would fight over the moon if they could.' She put her hand against Mellow's other cheek. 'But dear Mellow, that is not all that is troubling you today, is it?' The Hoopoe bird's feathers did not hold their usual lustre and it worried her.

'It is the Peewee birds,' Mellow replied. 'They all had the same strange dream.'

'All twenty-five of them?'

Mellow nodded and the golden feathers on his head swayed as if stroked by a soft breeze. 'As far as I can recall it has never happened before. Not just here in the Forest of Birds but anywhere in the Bird Kingdom.'

Oriole sat back. 'You taught me that dreams can show us the way forward. What is the meaning of their dream?'

'Hmm . . . I need time to think about it,' Mellow

replied. 'Meanwhile, why don't you sing us one of your early morning songs? It would cheer me up immensely.'

Oriole smiled. Singing was her most favourite thing to do. 'This one came to me last night as I was falling asleep,' she said. 'Let me see now . . . how did it begin . . . ah yes. I have called it "Song of the Wishbird" and it is for you, dear Mellow.'

The Song of the Wishbird rang out in the clear morning air. The birds of the Forest flew to the ancient Banyan tree and sat in rows, listening in rapt silence. Even Redbill and Droplet – who had begun quarrelling again – stopped and lifted their heads.

Oriole's song was about the rocks carved into strange shapes by the Wind, about the birds whose chorus filled every space in the Forest, about Fern Pond's icy waters that bubbled up from the centre of the earth. And about her love for Mellow, the magical Wishbird who was older than the ancient Banyan tree itself.

As Oriole finished, the Wind danced around the roots of the old tree. It, too, was listening. Then it laughed and whirled up into the sky, carrying in its breath the last beautiful song note. And a tiny new seed.

A hush lay over the Forest when Oriole finished.

'That was beautiful, child,' Mellow said dreamily. And the birds all twittered and nodded in agreement.

It was easy for Oriole to make up songs about Mellow for she loved him more than anything in the whole world. It was Mellow who had raised her from a small baby and given her dreams so that she would learn about the Outside, the world beyond the Forest of Birds. It was Mellow who had taught her how to speak as humans do, although when she did speak it was always in a musical voice – for Oriole had never known another human. The birds and the animals of the Forest were her family. And they were all that she needed.

'How quiet the Forest is,' Mellow muttered, after the other birds had flown away. He looked at Oriole. 'I must go now and think.' And with a flutter of feathers the Wishbird took flight.

Oriole felt a sudden chill and wrapped her cloak of rainbow feathers tightly about her. The cloak had been a gift from the birds of the Forest for her tenth birthday. Each bird had plucked a feather from its body to use in the weaving of the cloak.

Oriole climbed to the ground and began walking the narrow path to Fern Pond. The orb-weaving spiders were rebuilding the webs that had been damaged in the night. Dew dotted each fine strand so that they looked like sparkling necklaces made from tiny diamonds. It was from their silk thread that Oriole wove her dresses.

'Good morning, Weavers,' Oriole said as she passed, and the spiders shook their gold and brown bodies in reply.

When she reached Fern Pond she washed her hands and face and entered a cavern in the rocks where she kept her supply of fruit, nuts, berries and roots. Grabbing a handful of berries she went back outside.

Usually the trees were alive with colour as birds, some with long trailing tail-feathers, darted through the canopy. But on this morning not a leaf stirred. An ominous stillness seemed to suspend time.

'How quiet the Forest is,' Oriole murmured to herself, repeating Mellow's haunting words.

As Oriole went about her daily chores digging for roots, collecting firewood and mending her nest, shadows seemed to stalk her. She could see them out of the corner of her eye, but when she turned they were no longer there.

That night Oriole had a strange dream.

She dreamed that she was in a city surrounded by high walls and towers. On a pile of wood sat a boy in ragged clothes. Oriole touched him on the shoulder, wanting to ask directions, but when the boy lifted his head she leapt back in horror. The boy had no mouth. Oriole screamed but no sound came out. She felt for her own mouth. It, too, was gone.

She woke, her heart thudding in her chest. It was just a dream, she reassured herself. But never before had she seen such a terrifying vision. *I must find Mellow and ask him what it means,* she decided.

Oriole found Mellow perched on Fire Rock, a distant expression on his face. She sat down beside him but did not speak. The Wishbird was pondering something important and Oriole knew not to disturb him during these moments.

At last Mellow spoke. 'Do you have a question, Oriole?' he said.

'I had a frightening dream, Mellow,' she replied.

'Tell me your dream, child.'

So Oriole told Mellow about the walled city of mouthless people and about the ragged boy and how she tried to scream but found she had no mouth.

The Hoopoe bird sighed and hung his head. 'The time has finally come then,' he said sadly.

Oriole's heart quailed at Mellow's grave tone.

'You know that I am old.'

'Yes, Mellow, older than the Forest, older than the ancient Banyan tree itself,' Oriole said.

'You also know that as a Wishbird it is my job to mend the broken threads of the world.'

Oriole nodded. She had heard this many times before. Wishbirds preserved the precious fabric of life.

'But what I have never told you is that I was once the Wishbird for a long line of kings.'

'Then why are you not with them now?' Oriole asked.

'I was sent away and forbidden to return.'

'But why?'

The last King of Pafir was mad with grief when he lost his only son. He ordered the forests in his Kingdom be cut down and all the birds killed. Music was forbidden. I was lucky. He let me escape . . .'

'But birds are the most beautiful creatures on earth. And everybody needs music. Without it our souls would die,' Oriole said, horrified.

'That is true, Oriole, and it is the very reason why the city eventually became known as the City of Soulless instead of the City of Solace. The people came to forget how to sing and laugh and love.' Mellow paused. 'This morning I was visited by the Wind. She brought me bad news. My King is dying and a huge Barbarian Army from the Savagelands is advancing upon the city. Soon it will be at the gates. And then . . .' Mellow turned away from Oriole. She gazed at his feathers and suddenly saw how dull and lifeless they had become. As if the colour was slowly leaching from them.

'What, Mellow? What is it?' she asked urgently.

Mellow shrugged. 'It will all be over.'

'I do not understand . . .' She had never heard the Wishbird talk like this before.

Mellow ruffled his feathers and let them settle. 'There is a thread, Oriole, a thread that binds me to the King as it has bound me to all the kings that went before him. But now he has turned his back on the city and his people, I feel that thread gradually weakening. When it breaks, the Wishbird dies and the fabric of life will be rent.'

Oriole could barely breathe. Tears sprang to her eyes. 'That cannot be, Mellow! You told me that Wishbirds can never die. Is there not a tree or root medicine that can cure you?'

'Dear child, this is an illness of the soul and mind, not of the body. No plant can cure it.'

'What then? There must be something . . . Where is the Kingdom of Pafir? Can we not go there to see the King?' Tears streamed down Oriole's cheeks and she brushed them away furiously.

'The Kingdom is far from the Forest of Birds and I am too weak to fly. And even if I could go, I could not help, for the soldiers of Pafir cannot withstand the strength of this huge Barbarian Army.'

Oriole sobbed, 'But if you die, Mellow, I would surely die too . . .'

Mellow turned to her. 'My child,' he said calmly and quietly. 'We have passed twelve springs together and in that time I have taught you all that you need to know. Remember that.'

Oriole put her arms around her beloved Wishbird, leaning her forehead against his golden crest. It had always been the two of them, her and Mellow. This life was all she ever wanted, all she had ever known, and she thought it would be like this forever.

But in a day, in an instant, everything had changed.

3
THE TEST

The shack where Boy lived with Panther and Rabbit was built from rough planks of wood tacked together with rope and rusty nails. The wind whipped through it in winter and the boys sweltered in the summer, but it was their home. Behind the shack rose the city wall, so thick that a squad of soldiers could march four abreast along its top.

When Boy turned the corner into Ratskin Alley he saw Rabbit stirring a pot on a low coal-burning stove. Then he smelled something delicious.

'You're here,' said the older boy, rubbing his nose with the back of his hand and leaving a smudge of coal dust across his cheek. Rabbit was tall and lanky with large ears and a light growth of downy hair above his top lip.

'That smells like *real* meat, Rabbit,' Boy said. 'What are we celebrating?'

'Panther said to cook you somethin' nice, so that's what I'm doing . . . mutton an' turnips an' your favourite chilli noodles,' Rabbit replied, grinning.

'For me?' Boy was confused.

'Boy!' came a gruff voice from inside the shack. 'Get in here.'

Rabbit squatted down and began to fan the coals to bring up the heat. 'You better go. He's been waitin' for you all afternoon,' he said with a sympathetic nod towards the door.

Boy grinned and jingled the coin purse in his pocket as if to say, *Don't worry about me.*

As soon as he was inside, Panther pounced. 'Where you been?' he demanded, his words ripping through Boy's body like jagged claws.

Panther was the oldest of the three boys. He was lean with a high forehead and intense dark eyes.

'I was walking,' Boy replied.

'Don't you know there are plenty of bullies on the lookout for mugs like you? You're an easy target with your sleeves bulging with loot.'

'I was being followed, so I had to hide,' Boy lied. 'I got a nice haul, though. You want to see, Panther?'

Panther lifted his chin and looked down his nose at Boy. He tugged at a metal ring in his earlobe, a habit he had whenever he needed to think. A moment went by. Boy stared straight ahead, not daring to look into Panther's eyes.

'All right,' Panther said at last. 'Show me what you got.'

Boy dug into his pocket and pulled out the drawstring purse. He dropped it onto an upturned barrel that served as a table. The coins inside made a satisfying metallic *clunk*.

'Well, well,' Panther said, looking at the fullness of the bag. He tipped the coins out and began counting them. 'You did good today, Boy. Real good. There's enough money here to last us through the winter.'

Boy smiled.

'Food's ready!' Rabbit said as he pushed open the door and carried in three steaming plates. The smell of mutton stew filled the small shack.

Boy's mouth watered. Meat was a rare treat. He sat down on the dirt floor ready to eat.

'What we celebrating tonight, Panther?' Rabbit asked.

'Boy's test,' Panther said, putting a juicy piece of meat into Boy's bowl.

Boy looked up. 'Test?' he gulped. Suddenly he had lost his appetite.

'I want to see if you really are the best thief in the City of Soulless,' Panther said.

'But we already know that, Panther,' Rabbit said, grinning at Boy like a proud older brother.

'What do I have to do for the test?' Boy asked.

'Steal one of the Demon Monster's treasures,' Panther said, close to Boy's ear.

Boy's bowl slipped from his hand. He looked at Rabbit. Rabbit's face had gone white and his lips trembled. 'You want . . . you want Boy to go to the Demon Monster's mansion? But Panther, you know –'

Panther interrupted. 'Everyone knows the Demon Monster has a mansion full of treasures, but no one's ever been inside –'

'That's 'cos he eats children live,' whined Rabbit. 'Rips

their heads right off with his bare hands, then fries –'

Panther cuffed him across the ear.

Rabbit fell silent, rubbing the side of his face.

Boy was as brave as any boy could be, but just hearing the name 'Demon Monster' made him prickle with fear. Some said the Demon Monster was a serpent with eyes at both ends of his body. Others said that he looked like a man, but he had lost his head in battle so he carried it under his arm. Boy's stomach felt like a nest of seething ants.

'One little treasure is all we'd need,' Panther went on. 'Just think, Boy. We could eat like this every night. Rabbit could set up his own stand and cook his specialties just like he's always wanted. And you . . . you would never have to light-finger again.'

Boy shook his head. 'I can't, Panther,' he said, his voice trembling. 'Please don't make me.'

Panther breathed in deeply, then let out a long disappointed sigh. Boy knew what was going to come next.

'Who saved you from the Song Stealer's Cart?' Panther said. His voice had taken on a sing-song quality.

'You did, Panther.'

'And who gave you food and shelter and trained you to light-finger?'

Boy looked down at his spilled dinner. 'I'll bring you back a bigger money purse tomorrow and you can give me a beating, too,' he said.

Panther sighed again and stood up. 'You don't leave me much choice, do you, Boy?'

Boy hunched his shoulders, bracing himself for the beating. In the corner of the shack, leaning against the wall, stood the bamboo rod. But instead of picking it up, Panther knelt down and flipped over Boy's bedding. He began digging in the dirt. Boy bit his lip to stop crying out as Panther turned triumphantly with something in his hands. It was Boy's treasure box.

Rabbit looked from the box to Boy and back again. 'What is it?' he asked, confused.

'Just some things I kept,' Boy whispered.

'Kept?' Panther boomed. He turned the box upside down and Boy's treasures fell in the dirt. 'Looks like our Boy's not been too honest, Rabbit.'

'They're not valuable, not to anyone but me,' said Boy, feeling helpless.

'Seems to me they'd be valuable to their owners,' Panther said. 'Whose to say they wouldn't pay to have their precious things back?'

Boy suddenly remembered the silver box in his sleeve and crossed his arms over his chest.

Panther cocked his head on one side. 'What you got hidden up there, eh?'

Boy broke out in a cold sweat. 'Nothing, Panther. Honest.'

Grabbing hold of Boy's arm, Panther twisted it up and back so that Boy fell to his knees. 'Listen,' he said, his voice like tight wire. 'I'll tell you what I'll do. You can keep your precious things, including whatever's up your sleeve, but in exchange you do this job for me.'

Boy glanced up at Rabbit for help but the older boy had turned away. Boy looked at his treasures, glinting in the dirt, and his heart twisted. He couldn't let Panther take them, especially not his latest precious find.

'I'll do it. I'll do it . . .' he grunted with pain.

'Good,' said Panther, letting him up. 'Now, let's finish dinner.'

The stew was cold and Boy was not hungry any more. A moth fluttered towards the candle flame, its delicate wings about to catch on fire. Boy waved it away, holding back his tears. He would never cry in front of Panther, no matter how much he hurt him.

'You'll go tomorrow, then,' Panther said, and with that he caught the moth in his hand and crushed it.

4
THE WALLED CITY OF NIGHTMARES

Day after day Mellow's feathers began to lose their lustre. His eyes grew dull, his breath quickened, and there was nothing Oriole could do. The silence in the Forest had deepened, too. She rarely saw the other birds. Where had they gone?

One afternoon, when she was lying sadly in her nest, Redbill and Droplet alighted on a nearby branch.

'Oriole,' Redbill sang. 'There may be a way of saving our Mellow.'

Oriole sat up. 'How, Redbill? Why have you waited so long to tell me?'

'Because the way is fraught with danger,' Droplet said. He glanced at Redbill who nodded back at him solemnly.

'*We* cannot enter the City of Solace or we will be

killed,' Droplet went on. 'But you, Oriole . . . you being a girl may not be noticed. You must find the King and tell him that our Mellow is dying.'

Oriole's heart gave a lurch. 'But I have never left the Forest before. How will I get there. How will I know the way?'

'Show her, brother,' Droplet said. 'Show her now.' There was a tinge of excitement in his voice.

Redbill whistled loudly, a sound that carried deep into the heart of the Forest. Oriole looked at him, confused. How oddly the birds were behaving.

Then there came the beating of hundreds of wings. Oriole looked up. Above the Forest canopy, shimmering and winking in the afternoon sun, floated a strange coloured cloud. As it drew nearer, Oriole gasped. It wasn't a cloud but a tapestry woven from leaves and feathers spun together with spiders' silk and held in the Peewee birds' beaks.

The birds landed on the Banyan tree, letting the tapestry drape over the branches.

'We have been weaving it for days,' said Yellowspot, leader of the Peewee birds.

'So that is why the Forest has been so quiet and why I could not find you,' Oriole laughed. 'It is beautiful, but what is it for?'

'With this tapestry we will carry you to the city,' said Yellowspot.

'Carry me?' Oriole looked closely at the beautiful carpet and her heart sank. 'Are you strong enough to fly such a distance?'

'Of course we are,' said the Peewee birds in unison.

'We are ready to leave straightaway,' Redbill chirped.

'We can go most of the way with you,' said Purplewing, reassuringly.

'Please, Oriole. You are the only one who can save Mellow,' said Droplet.

The birds shuffled nervously, waiting for Oriole to speak. There was a long silence as she looked out over the Forest, her world of trees and quiet waters, of rocks and endless green. Then she looked at Mellow lying by Fern Pond, so still it was as if he was already dead, and grief and dread settled like a heavy stone in her belly. *It is up to me to save Mellow. Nobody else can do it.*

She turned to the birds and nodded slowly. They fluffed their feathers and jumped around on the branches in excitement.

'But first I must say goodbye to Mellow.' Oriole wrapped her cloak of rainbow feathers around her and climbed to the ground. When she reached the spot where Mellow lay, the birds who were tending him flew up to the trees so that she and the Wishbird could be alone.

'Mellow,' Oriole whispered.

Mellow's eyes fluttered.

'I am leaving now for the City of Solace. I am going to find your King.'

'No . . . Oriole. You must not go . . .' Mellow tried to get up, but he was too weak.

Oriole looked at her friend sadly. 'Goodbye, dear Mellow.' She leaned forward and kissed him on the cheek. And before he could say another word, she was gone.

Mellow had taught Oriole how to receive his dreams. This was the way he taught her about the Outside. When he told her a story, she would open her mind and visions would appear. In this way she knew the form of many things outside the Forest of Birds without ever having left it. But when the birds soared in the air pulling the tapestry behind them, Oriole never imagined the world to be so vast. How beautiful everything was. She felt like she was the Wind, dipping and soaring and swirling.

They flew over a cluster of turquoise lakes that mirrored the white fluffy clouds above her. There was no time to rest and the birds travelled through the night, taking it in turns to pull the tapestry.

The following day, the warm morning sun woke Oriole. She threw off her cloak of rainbow feathers and sat up. In front of her, a dark stain spread across the horizon. Oriole was seized by a cold dread. She knew instantly that this was the city of her nightmare, the city of mouthless people.

The birds lowered the tapestry gently to the ground. They were exhausted, but more than that she could sense they were deeply worried for her.

'We must leave you here. We cannot go any further, Oriole,' Redbill said. 'When you wish to return, send us a message with the Wind.'

'And please be careful,' the Peewee birds sang together.

Oriole sniffed back tears. She looked at her friends and wondered when she would see them again. Mellow had said that he had taught her all she needed to know. But was it going to be enough? In all her life she had never met another man, woman or child. She had never been into a city, never walked along roads, never been so afraid before.

But she could not let her friends know how scared she felt, so she lifted her chin and smiled and said, 'I will seek out the King and save our Mellow. Now off you go, dear ones, back to the Forest.'

While the birds gathered up the tapestry of woven leaves and feathers, Oriole turned and began to walk.

It was not until she heard the whoosh of departing wings did her tears fall like winter leaves from the ancient Banyan tree.

5

THE STRANGE GIRL

While Oriole stood at the gates of the City of Soulless, the wind howled around the shack at the bottom of Ratskin Alley. Boy was tossing and turning, dreaming about the Demon Monster. He often heard the city walls whispering, but tonight they seemed to be crying out in pain. *If only I could hold back tomorrow,* he thought.

But only Xi He, Goddess of the Sun, can stop night turning into day. And so the morning light came, like a pale ghost creeping through the cracks of the shack.

Boy looked across at Panther and Rabbit, lying on their backs and snoring. Rabbit would be the first one up, but not until the gong of the first daylight watch.

Boy quickly tied back his hair with a strip of frayed cloth and stepped outside. The air was foul with the stench of refuse strewn along the alleyway. A scrawny dog, with ribcage showing through tawny fur, skulked off when it spied him.

Where Ratskin Alley crossed Pickle Lane, Boy turned right to the market square. Panther had decided that market day, with its crowds of people, would be the perfect time for Boy to climb over the wall without being noticed.

The City of Soulless had begun as a small town, walled for protection from bandits. Over a thousand or more years, as the city grew, new walls were built and the old inner walls began to crumble and decay. There were four gates but only one was used and it was usually locked. This was not to keep strangers out, but to keep the people in, for nobody was allowed to leave the city without the King's permission. Some had tried, but they were all caught. And then they disappeared.

The Northern Gate was always heavily guarded. But once every month, like a fresh wind blowing from across the desert, traders from the Borderlands were allowed entry to the city to sell their wares – vegetables, fruits and spices, cloth, clothing and handicrafts, tools, furniture, pots and pans. It was a chaotic day of noise and smells and different languages. And for that one day every month Boy could feel a stirring of something close to happiness in the people around him.

Boy always looked forward to market day, but this morning his stomach heaved and his legs felt weak.

The place was already bustling with people setting up their stalls. Shelters of woven cane were strung between posts hammered into the dirt. Men with baskets swinging from each end of a bamboo pole carried on their shoulders trotted past huge melons sitting on the ground like the heads of green giants. Gourds, cabbages, lotus roots and radishes were displayed in baskets.

In another section were the stalls of the cloth merchants. The cloth merchants were only allowed to sell colours that were dull and dark – browns, greys, blues and blacks. It was all that the townspeople wore. But Boy had heard these desert merchants groan about their carts, sitting outside the gates, full of beautiful, brightly patterned materials that were banned in the City of Soulless.

Once, Boy had seen a trader try to smuggle in some cloth trimmed with aqua and orange. He had been thrown out by the guards. Then, at the last full moon, Rabbit said someone had smuggled in an instrument made from the wood of the dragon-blood tree. Boy didn't know what an instrument was, but it was obviously something dangerous for it was seized and burned in the Courtyard of the King.

As Boy walked down the main street that led to the market square, he heard the sound of horses and the rumble of wagon wheels. He quickly stepped out of the way as the wagon pulled up alongside him. A camel was sitting in the middle of the road, refusing to get up. The soldiers guarding the wagon ran on ahead, shouting at the camel's owner to move, and Boy turned to look at the strange wagon.

It was drawn by two horses and painted black, with four flags mounted on the roof. There was also a small barred window. Boy had never seen anything like it before, but for some strange reason he began to shake with fear.

Then a shadow stirred inside, and the face of a girl appeared behind the bars. She looked to be only a few years older than Boy with long dark hair and brilliant green eyes that darted about fearfully. Finally they came to rest on Boy's face.

The girl's hands came up to the bars and she gripped them tightly. Her mouth was bound with a cloth but her eyes pleaded for help.

Boy wanted to help her but there was nothing he could do. Then a beautiful sound came from the girl's throat. It was strange, and yet familiar too.

All at once Boy felt a tingling sensation envelope his

body and an image rose in his mind. It was the same face he had seen when he had touched the precious treasure in the silver box. This time the woman was sitting tall and straight, her hands gracefully lifting and falling, her head slightly tilted forward.

'Get away from there!' a soldier yelled, pushing Boy with such force that he fell into the gutter. The image was shattered.

The wagon moved on with a clatter and the girl was gone. Boy got to his feet and stood, quivering, on the side of the road.

'You get a look at that girl in the Song Stealer's Cart?' a woman standing nearby murmured. 'Haven't seen one of those carts in years.'

Song Stealer's Cart! Boy thought. *The same cart that took my ana and ata away . . .*

'They say she has the singing tongue,' the woman went on.

'What's that?' Boy asked, still dizzied by an urge to run after the cart.

'Some kind of illness left over from before the Fell,' the woman said. 'There were a lot who had it in those days. But they're all gone now. We can't have that kind of sound in the city . . . stops people from working . . .'

She trailed off, looking confused, as if she had forgotten what she was talking about.

'Where are they taking her?' Boy asked.

'The Palace dungeon, I suppose. Then she'll disappear, like the rest of them.'

Boy looked down the road. The King's Palace sat behind its own great stone wall. The Song Stealer's Cart, just a small black speck now, stood waiting for the Palace gates to open.

Boy's mouth had gone dry. He swallowed but no saliva came. The sound of the girl's voice and the sight of the Song Stealer's Cart had stirred something deep inside him, evoked a memory of a long ago past.

Could that girl lead me to my ana and ata? he wondered.

He took a step towards the Palace and an image of Panther rose before him, Boy's treasures crushed carelessly in his hands.

Boy faltered, then turned away.

First he would go to the Demon Monster's mansion.

Then, if he got out alive, he would find the girl with the singing tongue.

6
INTO SOULLESS

The land surrounding the City of Solace was devoid of all life. Oriole saw dead tree stumps, hundreds of them stretching all the way to the grey city walls.

At first she could not understand what had happened. Then she realised with sudden horror that each stump had axe marks cut clean and sharp into the wood. This had once been a mighty forest.

As the walls towered above her, Oriole felt a sadness emanating through every brick, oozing like blood from a festering wound. Along the top were battlements and watchtowers and soldiers wearing metal helmets and carrying crossbows.

Oriole was aware of eyes staring down at her as she walked up to the huge wooden gates. A soldier nodded to someone below and one half of the gate opened. A puff of foul air escaped from within. Mellow had told her that humans were unpredictable, that they could be smiling at you and offering their hand while thinking of a way to attack. Oriole tried to stay calm.

'Where are you from and what goods do you have to sell?' a soldier asked, brusquely.

Oriole looked at him in surprise. It was not what he said, she understood the words, but his voice was strange and flat – there were no highs or lows and each word ran into the other.

The soldier looked Oriole up and down and frowned at her cloak of rainbow feathers. 'Out with it! I haven't got all day.'

'Please, Sir,' Oriole replied in her bird-like singing voice. 'I would like to see the King.'

The guard stepped back, his eyes wide. Then he found his voice and pointed. 'Seize her. She has the singing tongue!'

At once Oriole was surrounded by soldiers with their swords drawn. Two of the men grabbed her by the arms. Oriole had only ever known the softness of feathers against her cheek, the brush of leaves against her legs, the gentle stirring of the Forest. But the soldiers' rough hands felt like thorny bark and her ears ached from the shouting. She began to tremble.

'Please let me go,' she said. 'I have come to see —'

A soldier covered her mouth with his hand as if her words were poison. His fingers smelled of dead things. They gagged her with a dirty rag and tied her hands behind her back. Then she was led through the city.

A crowd began to gather. They gawked and pointed. 'Singing tongue. She's got the singing tongue,' they said in their strange monotonous voices.

The road was flanked by wooden buildings crowded one on top of the other. Everything in the City of Soulless seemed cold and grey and hostile.

Oriole was forced into the back of a horse-drawn cart. There was a small barred window that let in some light. The door slammed shut and Oriole looked out at the people staring back at her. Their eyes were dull, their faces expressionless. No one laughed or smiled. There was the smell of decay everywhere; not the earthy decay of leaves and wood like in her beloved Forest of Birds, but the decay of dead things. It poured from the houses. It was on people's breath. Oriole sank to the cart floor and covered her face.

The cart came to a sudden halt. The horses stamped their feet, hooves echoing on stone. Oriole stood up and peered out through the bars.

It was then that she saw the boy.

His clothes were patched and his hair held back with a piece of frayed cloth.

I know you! she thought. *You are the boy from my dream.*

And all at once it was as if she had found a friend. There was something different about him. It was his eyes, yes . . . they were alive, as if a small fire burned inside.

Oriole wanted to speak to him, but it was impossible with her mouth bound tight, so she pleaded with her eyes. Pleaded for him to help her.

Then she realised that the gag did not stop her from humming. She gathered all her hope and began to hum.

The boy looked startled, then the corners of his mouth turned up into a smile and he stared in a kind of rapture. He stepped towards her and Oriole's heart lifted.

Suddenly a guard appeared and threw the boy to the ground, shouting. Before he could get to his feet the cart had clattered forwards and Oriole lost sight of the only person who could rescue her. She sank to the floor again, helpless, as the Song Stealer's Cart rumbled on.

Oriole was still sitting on the floor when the cart stopped and the door finally swung open. A big man with a finely trimmed beard scowled at her and jerked his head, silently ordering her to get out. He wore a robe of fine purple cloth, with coloured beads adorning the collar and cuffs. He looked more like a beautiful bird from a forest than the dull grey townspeople.

He must be important, thought Oriole. *Maybe he is the King!* She felt suddenly hopeful again.

But as she stepped down the man snatched her cloak of rainbow feathers from her shoulders and threw it to the ground. Oriole shivered without it. She wore only a dress of spiders' silk and on her feet were thin shoes the birds had woven from vines.

'What do you want me to do with it, Lord Chancellor?' the soldier asked as he picked up the cloak and held it away from his body in disgust.

'Follow me. We are going to see the King,' said the man. His voice was cold and grey, worse than any of the voices she had heard so far, and it filled her with dread.

Oriole followed the Lord Chancellor's flowing purple robes across a courtyard and into a huge building. One of the dreams she had received from Mellow was of a beautiful palace with high ceilings and walls covered with murals of birds and forests and ladies walking along paths edged with flowers. But in this palace the paint was peeling and the walls were cracked. Only if she looked carefully could she see the scenes that Mellow had given her, like snatches of a fading dream.

The Lord Chancellor led Oriole into a hall empty of

all furniture except a throne on a stone dais. Behind the throne hung a heavy cloth with a forest hunting scene. It, too, was torn and faded.

'Tell the King to come at once,' the Lord Chancellor ordered one of the soldiers.

Except for the Lord Chancellor's loud breathing, all was quiet as they waited for the King to arrive. The cold that came up from the stone floor made Oriole shiver uncontrollably.

Soon this dreadful ordeal will be over. I will tell the King how far I have come, how ill Mellow is, and everything will be better, she thought.

7

THROUGH THE HOLE
IN THE WALL

The wall of the Demon Monster's mansion bordered the market place where the cloth merchants laid out their wares.

'Want your fortune read?' an old woman asked Boy.

Boy shook his head and slipped behind her. He studied the wall. He had to find a way to get over it, but it was very high and smooth. There was nowhere to place your feet or hold on to.

The old woman spoke again, her voice thickly accented with tones from the Grasslands. 'If you never ask, you will never find out,' she said, folding her fabrics and laying them in neat piles on the ground. Blues in one pile, greys in another, browns in the third. She stood up and smoothed back her wispy grey hair, adjusting a headband that was embroidered with dancing horses. 'Remember this, son. It is not up you want, but down.'

Boy turned and looked at her, puzzled.

The old woman leaned forward and whispered in his ear, 'In darkness seek the light. In stillness is motion.' Then she turned away to serve a customer.

How strange, Boy thought. 'Not up, but down,' he repeated.

He bent down on one knee and felt behind the weeds that grew along the bottom of the wall until he found a small depression. He pushed his hand further in and met no resistance.

There was a hole! It was not big enough for him to crawl through – he would have to work at making it larger. But the market place was too busy now. He stood up to think. And the old woman's other words flashed through his mind.

In darkness seek the light.

Boy shook his head. *I can't come back when it's dark. It's scary enough in daylight.* And yet the lady's words were insistent, prodding him . . .

In darkness seek the light. In darkness seek the light.

Boy grimaced. There was no other way.

The street sweepers, their twig brooms laid across wheelbarrows of rubbish, were leaving. The market square lay silent and empty. Dark clouds gathered overhead.

Boy found the spot in the wall where he had felt the hole earlier that day and began kicking it with his foot. Pieces crumbled away easily and before long the hole was big enough for him to crawl through. Vines that had crept inside tugged at his clothes as if to hold him back, to warn him of danger. But he pulled forward, until his head was through the wall.

What Boy didn't expect on the other side was a garden — a garden thick with trees. From the market square, you couldn't see them at all. But here they were, towering above him, reaching to the blackened sky. And they seemed to be murmuring to him as their branches rubbed together. The murmuring was drowned out by a rumble of thunder.

Boy touched a tree trunk, feeling the roughness of the bark against his palm. The only trees in the City of Soulless were short stunted bushes. He had never seen anything as tall as these. He put his nose to the wood and breathed. It smelt so sweet. Rain hitting the top of his head made him look up. A flash of lightning illuminated the black sky. When he looked back at the forest it seemed darker than ever.

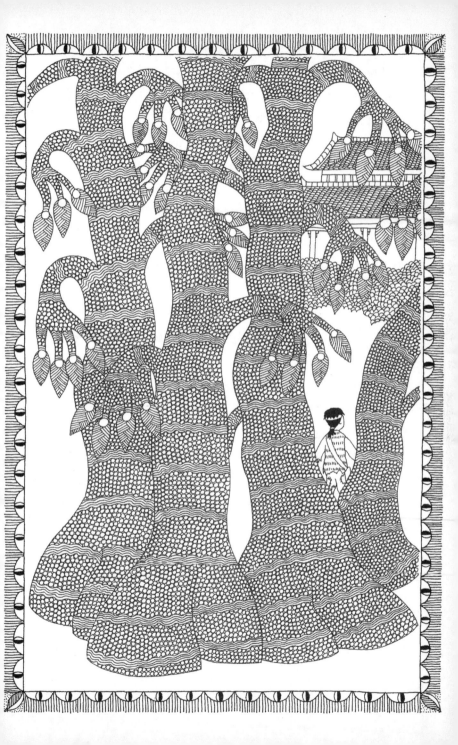

Then he spied a tiny light. It danced and disappeared and reappeared. Was it a firefly? He couldn't tell if it was near or far away, or if it was big or small.

His heart began drumming in his ears. Keeping the light in sight he set off along a winding track.

The trees opened up abruptly. On the other side of the clearing, revealed in a flash of lightning, was a house with a candle flickering in the window. Boy drew in a shivery breath as he looked at the Demon Monster's mansion.

Another fork of lightning rent the sky and he spied something out of the corner of his eye. He realised suddenly that he was surrounded by four huge statues: a tiger, a tortoise, a dragon, and a strange creature with many limbs.

But wait. Did that tiger just move? Boy turned around very slowly to face it.

The tiger, which appeared to be made of stone, was definitely not where it had been standing in the last lightning flash. Boy heard a roar followed by a booming peal of thunder. The thunder seemed to awaken the dragon from its sleep. It stirred and Boy stumbled backwards. Then the tortoise stretched out its neck. Only the many-limbed creature remained still.

Boy wanted to run, but in which direction? The wall was somewhere back through those dark trees. The house was closer. Either the Demon Monster would eat him or the figures would. He took off towards the light as fast as he could. But as he passed the strange creature it too began to move. Then it leapt into the air, claws extended, eyes blazing.

Boy froze as the terrifying beast hovered above him. There was no escaping it. All he could do was hunch down with his arms over his head. He closed his eyes tight, waiting for the attack.

Suddenly there was silence. The thunder had ceased. Boy opened his eyes and looked around. The four monsters were statues again, each one sitting quietly on its plinth. Had he imagined it all?

Letting out a long breath of relief, Boy stood up.

A cold hand gripped his shoulder. Then a rope fell around his neck.

8

THE IMPRISONED MOON

Footsteps sounded in the wide hallway. The King, wearing a long orange robe with a plaited black sash at his waist, entered the room flanked by five men. He was a tall man with a straight nose and broad mouth, but his skin looked grey and his shoulders drooped.

'Kowtow before the King!' the Lord Chancellor ordered Oriole. She knelt down and touched the floor with her forehead like the soldiers around her.

Aided by one of the men, the King mounted the dais and sat down on the throne. 'Who is this girl?' he asked. His voice was weak and his breathing laboured, as if he had not the strength even to talk. Oriole thought of Mellow and the thread that bound him to the King.

'She has the singing tongue, Your High One,' said the

Lord Chancellor in a grave tone.

'Take off the gag and let her speak for herself,' the King ordered.

As soon as the cloth was removed Oriole looked up at the King and said, 'Please . . . Your High One. I have journeyed from the Forest of Birds –'

The King's eyes grew wide and he raised his arm to stop her. He began to cough.

'How dare you use the singing tongue in the presence of The High One!' the Lord Chancellor said.

'I am sorry, but I cannot speak in any other way,' Oriole said, confused.

At that moment the doors burst open and a soldier rushed into the room. He removed his helmet and bent down on one knee before the King.

'I have urgent news, Your High One. A messenger has ridden from the borders of our Kingdom. An army led by Big Mo Ding of the Savagelands is on its way to the city and is destroying everything in its path. What are your orders?'

The King rubbed his temples. 'What do you advise, General?'

The Lord Chancellor stepped forward. 'Your High One, if I may interrupt. I have heard that Big Mo Ding is not as ruthless as is rumoured providing he meets no resistance. I suggest you send a messenger to meet him and agree to a pact. Perhaps you could offer him the low-producing eastern corner of the Kingdom in return for sparing the city.'

The General frowned. 'I beg to differ, Lord Chancellor,' he protested. He turned back to the King. 'We must act now. Big Mo Ding will stop at nothing to capture the whole Kingdom. We will be at his mercy like pigs to the slaughter.'

'General,' the Lord Chancellor snapped, 'you have allowed our army to grow fat and lazy. If you had done your job and trained –'

The General flushed with anger, but the King raised his hand before he could reply. He gave a rasping cough then said, 'Both of you, stop this bickering. I am tired. Leave now and take that girl to the dungeon. The sound of her singing tongue has made my head ache.'

'At once, Your High One,' the Lord Chancellor said. He glanced at the General and Oriole was startled to see an ugly sneer flash across his face. Then he bowed low before the King.

'No, wait, please . . . you have to help . . .' Oriole tried to speak, but the cloth was tied around her mouth again and she was escorted from the hall.

As soon as they were around the corner, the Lord

Chancellor did a strange thing. He pulled aside one of the guards and whispered in his ear. Now, Oriole's hearing was better than any human's. Having lived all her life in the forest, she was sensitive to sound. She could even hear conversations between the insects in their tunnels underground.

'Send a rider out to Big Mo Ding's camp,' she heard the Lord Chancellor whisper. 'Tell him the King is very weak. It won't be long before he surrenders. Wait a few days, then attack. The city will be easily taken.'

Oriole was confused. *If Big Mo Ding is the enemy, why is the Lord Chancellor sending him this message?* When the Lord Chancellor turned towards her, she pretended to be looking out of the window, her thoughts churning.

They crossed several courtyards to the back of the Palace grounds. Then she was dragged down a flight of curling steps.

An old guard met them at the door. When he saw the Lord Chancellor he looked surprised. The old guard straightened his clothes, smoothed back his hair and bowed.

'What is your name?' the Lord Chancellor asked.

'I am Old Ardi,' the guard replied.

'Well, Old Ardi, the King has ordered this girl's tongue be cut out.'

Oriole gasped and shook her head. She wanted to speak, to tell the guard that the Lord Chancellor was lying, but the gag was tight about her mouth. Old Ardi seemed surprised.

'Do it or suffer the same punishment,' the Lord Chancellor said threateningly.

'Yes, of course, Lord Chancellor.'

Old Ardi bowed and stepped away. The Chancellor turned and stalked back up the steps.

When they were alone, Old Ardi pulled off the strip of cloth and mumbled, 'Whatever have you done, child?'

Oriole wanted to tell him that the King had ordered no such thing. She wanted to say that the Lord Chancellor was a dishonourable man, that he was siding with the enemy, but she was too afraid to speak. Every time she opened her mouth, something bad seemed to happen. She thought of Mellow waiting for her to return and a tear ran down her cheek.

Old Ardi shrugged sadly and led her down a long dark passage. He stopped outside one of the cells and pulled the door open. 'I suppose you're hungry,' he said, nodding for her to go inside. 'I'll get you something to eat.' He took a key on a long strip of leather from inside his vest and locked the door behind her.

A cockroach scuttled across the floor and slipped

through a tiny crack in the wall. Oriole wished she could escape as easily. She wrapped her arms around herself and felt her knees give way. A single window covered with bars was set up high in the ceiling. Barely any light touched the floor. How she longed to be home in the Forest up in her nest in the ancient Banyan tree with Mellow. As the square of light from the window above turned from yellow to pale grey, she realised it would soon be night. Oriole drifted to sleep, cold and scared.

A key in the lock jerked Oriole awake. It was Old Ardi.

'I brought you food and some clean straw to keep you warm. You must be cold in that thin dress of yours,' he said. He let the bundle of straw drop from under his arm and set the bowl on the ground.

Oriole remembered what Mellow had once told her. 'Actions make you who you are, not what you say or how you look.'

Old Ardi is a good man, she thought, as she peered down at the steaming bowl. In the Forest of Birds, she ate fruit, nuts, berries and roots. Some she cooked, others she ate raw. Mellow had told her that humans ate animals, but to her relief Old Ardi had not given her meat, but some sort of yellow grain in warm water.

The dungeon was dark and damp, but she felt her heart warm a little as she ate. And she still had her tongue. For now.

9
PRISONER OF A DEMON

Boy was poked and prodded into the house, the rope
still tight around his neck. In the darkness he had only
glimpsed a face. *At least the Demon Monster doesn't have
two heads or carry one of them under his arm,* he thought.

The Demon Monster pushed Boy down onto a stool.
He loosened the rope and tied the other end of it to the
table leg. Then he went to the stove to tend to a very large
clay pot cooking over the fire. Boy's stomach rolled when
the Demon Monster lifted the lid and the room filled
with the smell of meat stew. Could it really be children
he's eating? Boy's knees shook and his lips trembled.

The Demon Monster turned away from the stove and
Boy saw his face for the first time. He was surprised to
see how ordinary he looked. He wore a brown robe with

trousers tucked into high boots. There was a scar in the shape of a hook down his left cheek. Boy was sure he had seen one exactly like it before, but where?

The Demon Monster ladled some stew into a porcelain bowl and set it on the table in front of Boy.

'Eat!' he said.

'I . . . I'm not very hungry,' Boy said.

'Children are always hungry,' the Demon Monster replied. 'And have you forgotten your manners? When someone gives you food you should be thankful.'

'Yes, Uncle.' Boy picked up the spoon and fished around in the gravy, searching for the smallest bit of meat, but he knew it was no use. In the end he would have to eat every last piece. The Demon Monster sat at the opposite end of the table, watching him.

Boy ate slowly. 'Can I go now, please?' he said when he had finally finished.

There was no reply. The Demon Monster had fallen asleep!

Boy looked at the door. It was unlocked. Very slowly, he worked at loosening the rope around his neck. At last it was big enough to slip over his head. He rose silently from his chair and tiptoed to the door. But just as he was about to open it, he heard a strange sound coming from the inner part of the house, a sound that reminded him of the girl with the singing tongue. He stopped, entranced.

The scrape of a chair leg quickly snapped Boy back to reality. The Demon Monster was on his feet.

Boy ran out the door and did not stop running until he reached the wall. Then he crawled through the hole and ducked and weaved down the alleys until he was sure he wasn't being followed.

It had begun to rain again, so Boy took shelter beneath a piece of woven cane. He thought about what he was going to do next. *I can't go back to the shack, not without something for Panther.*

He tucked his knees under his chin and closed his eyes. Then he opened them again.

If I go to the Palace and look for the girl with the singing tongue, I might find a treasure there as well.

He stood up with sudden resolve.

10

THE GIRL WITH THE
SINGING TONGUE

Finding the treasure in the silver box and hearing the girl with the singing tongue had given Boy all kinds of strange and new feelings. He had only ever known Panther and Rabbit, the threats and the beatings, and the dirty shack at the bottom of Ratskin Alley. Now it was as if a crack had appeared in the grey cloud above the city and he could see the sun for the first time. Could this girl lead him to his ana and ata?

Boy ran quietly along the back lanes to the district known as the Perfumed Garden. It was not a real garden, for hardly any existed in the City of Soulless. It was just a place where waste from the Palace was disposed of.

When Rabbit was low on food, he would wait for the wagons to return so he could get first pickings.

Sometimes he found meat only slightly tinged with green. With a little washing the smell disappeared. It was Rabbit who had told Boy about the nightly routine of the rubbish wagons. At the sound of the gong of the second night watch, a wagon loaded with empty barrels would leave the Perfumed Garden and head for the Palace. After filling up with waste it would return at the last gong before dawn.

Boy was waiting for the wagon when the horses emerged, white clouds of steam blowing from their nostrils. As the wagon passed by he jumped onto the open tray, crawled to the back and crouched down between the barrels behind the driver. Boy's main worry was how to get off the wagon without being noticed. Rabbit had told him that the men always went inside the Palace kitchen first, so it was easy to sneak off unseen. Still, things could go wrong; Boy knew that only too well.

He heard the driver mumbling to himself – something about the girl and the Song Stealer's Cart. He strained to catch more, perhaps news about where she was being held prisoner, but it was impossible over the rumble of wheels on cobblestones.

Soon they were at the gates of the Palace. His hands began to sweat. If everything went to plan and he found the girl, he had to make sure he was on the wagon when it left just before dawn. As the gates opened he crouched down low between the barrels.

'I have to do a search,' he heard someone say.

'Go ahead,' the driver said lazily and slumped down in his seat, crossing his arms over his chest.

To Boy's horror, the guard came around the back of the wagon holding a burning torch in one hand and a sword in the other. He started to thrust the blade into the empty barrels and the dark spaces between. Boy pressed himself back between two barrels and closed his eyes. He felt the sword nick his arm and he had to resist the urge to cry out. Then it was gone.

'Move on,' said the guard grumpily.

The wagon rumbled forwards through the gates.

When it was a safe distance from the gate, Boy jumped off and ducked behind some huge stone steps. He crouched there in the dark, heart pounding, but no one shouted out. Cautiously he sidled around the side of the Palace.

At the back was a smaller stone building with slit windows and bars. *That must be the dungeon,* he thought. But to get to it he had to cross a courtyard patrolled by soldiers. He watched for a while and counted the time between patrols. Then he sunk down on his hands and knees and crawled lizard-like around the perimeter of the courtyard. Whenever a soldier passed close by, Boy held his breath. He had learned how to be so still as to be invisible. The secret was to hush all thoughts. So Boy made his mind go blank and the soldiers walked right on by.

Two guards stood at the entrance to the dungeon, talking. Boy slipped past them, searching for another way in. Then he saw a row of lights in the ground. He crept closer, wondering what they could be, and saw that they weren't lights at all but small, barred windows. When he looked through one of them, he saw that it belonged to a cell. Each small window had a cell beneath it. Boy grew excited.

He called softly down into the first one. 'Are you there, girl with the singing tongue?'

When there was no answer, he moved onto the next cell, and then the next. But each one seemed to be empty. Finally he arrived at the last cell. He peered down into the darkness and saw movement, briefly, in the corner.

'Don't be scared, girl with the singing tongue. It's me, the boy from the market place. Please come out.'

The girl stepped into the moonlight under the window and stared up at Boy.

'I remember you. You are the one with the fire in your eyes,' she said.

Boy stared down at her, unable to speak. Although he had heard her strange voice in the Song Stealer's Cart, he had never heard a language like this before. Each word rose and fell melodically. So this is what the woman meant when she spoke of a singing tongue.

Again the strange feeling of familiarity washed over him so that he had to close his eyes and cling tightly to the bars.

'Where do you come from?' he asked.

'The Forest of Birds,' the girl replied.

'I've never heard of that place. Where is it?'

'One flying day and a night away.'

Boy laughed. 'Flying day?'

'My friends, the birds, carried me here on a tapestry of leaves and feathers.'

Boy's face fell. 'Birds? What are they?'

'One day I will show you,' she said. 'I do not understand why I have been imprisoned. Please help me escape . . .'

But Boy's mind was on something else. Another memory stirred. 'I remember now. I've seen the Song Stealer's Cart before,' he said. 'When I was small I wanted to run after it but something . . . something terrifying made me run and hide instead.'

'Are you all right?' the girl asked, her eyes shining in the moonlight.

'The Song Stealer's Cart, the one that brought you here, it's the same cart that took my parents away a long time ago and I'm still looking for them. Have you seen any other prisoners here? Are there other people in the Forest of Birds?' He held his breath, waiting for her answer.

The girl shook her head. 'There are no people living in the Forest. And I have only met the King, who is gravely ill, and the Lord Chancellor, who appears to be a dishonest man.'

Boy sat back on his heels, disappointed. She knew nothing about his parents. And yet he had been so sure . . .

'I must return to the Forest of Birds. Will you help me get out of here?' she said urgently.

He bent down over the window again. 'I don't know if I can help you.'

'Oh, but you must! The guard has been ordered to cut out my tongue,' cried the girl softly, biting her lip.

Tears filled her eyes and Boy looked at her, aghast. 'Cut out your tongue? But that is horrible. Who would order such a thing?'

Then all at once he heard the rumbling wagon and was struck by an idea. He looked at the girl standing in the moonlight. Even though she couldn't help him find his ana and ata, he knew he couldn't leave her to such a terrible fate.

'I have an idea,' he said. 'Can you hold onto your

tongue until tomorrow night?'

'I will try,' she replied.

Boy turned to leave.

'Wait. I am Oriole. What is your name?' the girl asked.

'Boy.'

'Just Boy?'

'Yes, just Boy,' he said. And he ran off into the night.

11

THE TRICK OF
THE TONGUE

The smell of blood was thick in the air when Boy walked down Slaughter Alley. Butcher stalls lined both sides of the twisting street. Blowflies landed on hanging carcasses and on chunks of meat laid out on tables. The older pieces, ones with fat crawling maggots, were sold at cheaper prices.

Dawn crept into the city as Boy approached Butcher Tan's stall. Butcher Tan was a friend to Boy. He would often give him off-cuts and leftover bones to take back to Rabbit for a delicious noodle broth.

The meat seller was standing in front of the carcass of a large pig. 'You're up early, Boy,' he said. With one blow he chopped through the pig's hind leg.

'Do you have a sheep's tongue, Butcher Tan? I can't

pay for it, but I'll do errands for you in return,' Boy said.

Tan, a short man with a big belly, looked at Boy through half-closed eyes. 'Is Panther up to one of his tricks again?'

'No, Butcher Tan. It's not for Panther, it's for me. Well, not exactly for me . . . it's for a girl.' Boy felt himself blush.

'A girl, eh?' The butcher smiled. 'I won't ask any more questions, then.' He headed to the back and disappeared behind a row of hanging carcasses.

'Slaughtered the sheep this morning so her tongue is still good and fresh. It will be a tasty treat for your girl.' Butcher Tan returned holding a tongue around the middle. It looked like a pale pink fish in his hand.

'Can you chop it in half for me?' Boy asked.

Butcher Tan laid the tongue on his chopping block and cut the tongue in two. Then he wrapped it in a lotus leaf. 'There you go,' he said.

Boy placed it carefully into a bag slung across his shoulder and thanked the butcher for his kindness.

All through the day, Boy kept an eye out for Panther and Rabbit. He couldn't let himself be seen, not now, not when it was so vital to save Oriole before they cut out her tongue. But he had failed to steal something from the Demon Monster's mansion and he had not returned home. He knew that Panther would be fuming. Would

71

he destroy Boy's treasure box as punishment? Even thinking about him touching each tiny precious thing made Boy cringe. He would think of a way to get it back – he had to, it was all he had. But first he must free the girl with the singing tongue.

Deep in the Palace dungeons, Oriole sat huddled in despair. She had journeyed such a long way only to be imprisoned in this dark and terrible place. She had failed Mellow, failed the birds of the Forest and failed herself.

There came a sound from far away, a strange and comforting wind blew through the cell. It was almost like music. Oriole tilted her head and listened carefully, but it seemed to be coming from the walls themselves. She let the music wrap around her as she slept.

That night, after hitching a ride once again on the rubbish wagon, Boy waited for a chance to slip past the guards. Finally, when their backs were turned and they were deep in argument, he crept down the winding steps.

He had the tongue in his bag – the easy part of his

plan was complete. Now for the hard part.

At the bottom of the steps Boy turned a corner and almost fell over another guard. He was sitting on a stool, his legs outstretched, fast asleep. Boy looked around for the keys to unlock the cells. There was nothing hanging on the walls or lying on the table. *Where would the old guard keep them?* he wondered. Then he spied something that looked like metal, peeping out from the guard's vest.

Boy slowly withdrew the key which was attached to a long leather strap, but stopped when he saw something else. Tangled around the end of it was a small embroidered pouch with a bright orange tassel.

The old guard has a treasure of his own, thought Boy.

He opened the pouch. Two small silver bracelets – the kind a baby wore on both wrists to keep the Baby Snatching Spirit away – were wrapped in cloth. Boy looked at the old guard. Did he carry these treasures around inside his vest because his child had been taken away? Had he, too, lost someone?

For the first time in his life as a thief, Boy hesitated. Then he returned the treasure to its owner and set off down the corridor, looking for Oriole. Reed torches mounted along the walls made long flickering shadows dance across the ceiling. Boy's shadow was a tall young tree.

I might not need the tongue after all, he thought as he reached the last cell. *This is going to be easy.*

He whispered through the tiny peephole, 'Oriole! It's me, Boy. Are you there?'

When Oriole heard Boy's voice she ran to the door. 'Oh, you came back,' she said.

'Of course I came back,' Boy replied.

'Quickly,' Oriole whispered. 'I will surely die on the spot if I do not get out of here.'

'I see you still have your tongue,' Boy smiled, and inserted the key in the lock.

Oriole froze. 'Someone's coming,' she whispered.

Boy glanced around. The only place to hide was an alcove where the torchlight did not reach. It had iron rings and chains attached to the wall. Boy guessed it was where the prisoners were tortured. If he stood flush to the wall and very still he might not be seen. He leapt to the side as Old Ardi lumbered into sight.

'Now where did I put that key?' Old Ardi mumbled to himself. Then he spied it in the lock of Oriole's cell. 'I'm getting too old for this job,' he said, shaking his head.

Boy watched from the shadows as Old Ardi unlocked the door. He stopped in the entrance. 'I am sorry to have to do this, child,' he said. The guard had a long thin knife hidden behind his back.

Boy cried out. 'Wait!' he said, and stepped into the light.

Old Ardi reeled backwards with fright, dropping the knife. 'Who are you? What are you doing here,' he said in a shaky voice.

'Old Ardi, this is my friend Boy,' Oriole sang.

Old Ardi looked at Oriole in shock. It was the first time he had heard her speak.

'The singing tongue! Am I dreaming?' he said.

'I came to save Oriole,' Boy replied.

'There is no saving anyone who has the singing tongue. The Lord Chancellor himself came down this evening to see if I had carried out the King's command and said it must be done by dawn. I have no choice.'

'The King ordered no such thing,' said Oriole. 'The Lord Chancellor lied to you.'

Old Ardi looked at Oriole and then at Boy.

'Listen, Old Ardi,' said Boy. 'I know you don't want to hurt Oriole so I have come up with a plan.' He dipped into his bag and pulled out the tongue.

Oriole stepped back in disgust. 'What is that?'

'It's just a sheep's tongue,' said Boy. 'But it could look human if you put it in a box with some cloth around it. I don't think the Lord Chancellor will know the difference. What do you think?'

Old Ardi shook his head. 'I don't know if that would work. What's he going to say when he sees she has escaped?'

'That's easy,' said Boy. 'We'll make it look like Oriole fought you, knocked you to the ground and ran away. Then we'll escape on the rubbish wagon.'

'Please, Old Ardi,' Oriole said. 'I would rather you plunge that knife into my heart than never be able to sing again.'

Old Ardi looked down at Oriole's small face. She was so young. An innocent child. *What does it matter if I die?* he thought. *I am old.* And all at once a memory, a glimpse of how the city used to be, came to him. A memory of a time before the Fell. Old Ardi rubbed his brow. His head began to hurt. His hand crept inside his vest and touched the little embroidered pouch with the orange tassel that nestled against his skin. His heart grew lighter.

'No, you two, just go. I will invent something to tell the Lord Chancellor. You'd better follow me though. I'll take you out another way to catch the wagon.'

'Oh, thank you, Old Ardi,' Oriole said, and she stood on her tiptoes and gave him a kiss.

Before the last gong of dawn, two small shadows slipped unseen onto the rubbish wagon as it trundled out through the Palace gates.

12
BOY'S SECRET NEST

'Is this your nest?' Oriole asked, squeezing into the alcove that was barely big enough for one.

'I come here when I want to get away from Panther.' It was the first time Boy had shown anyone his hideaway in Burnt Water Lane.

Oriole's eyes widened. 'You live with a panther? Oh, I have only ever dreamed of those beautiful creatures.'

'Panther is not a real panther,' said Boy, smiling, confused. 'That's just his name. And he is not beautiful.'

'If we were in the Forest of Birds,' said Oriole, 'I would weave you a garland from the leaves of the ancient Banyan tree and you would wear it around your head so that all the creatures would know you are brave and strong.'

Boy felt his face redden. Luckily it was dark in the

alcove. Nobody had ever called him *brave* before. 'It was Panther who raised me. Rabbit lives with us too,' he said.

'I also have no parents,' Oriole said, wistfully. 'Mellow raised me. He's a Wishbird. He taught me the language of humans and told me stories and gave me dreams about how good and how bad humans can be.'

'You keep talking about birds, but I still don't understand what they are,' Boy said. He never tired of listening to her sing-song voice.

'They are the most wonderful of all creatures. They have wings that are like arms that lie beside their bodies, and when they stretch them out they can fly. Why, they are such wonderful fliers there is no match for them in all the world.'

'Are they like insects then?' Boy said, trying to make a picture in his mind.

'Birds are warm to touch; insects are cold. Birds have beating hearts like we do but feathers all over their bodies.'

'I hope I will see a bird one day,' said Boy.

Oriole felt tears forming. She had come such a long way and had only succeeded in getting herself put in prison. 'I came here to speak with the King so that I might save Mellow, for he is ill. But that has all gone wrong. I do not know what to do now.'

'There must be some other way to save your Mellow,'

Boy said, trying to comfort her. 'I am the best light-finger in Soulless. I know a lot of people and hear things. I can ask around.'

'Light-finger? What is that?'

'I steal things from people's clothing without them knowing,' Boy said proudly.

'Oh, that sounds like a game I play with Mellow! He hides things and I hunt for them. He says it improves my powers of thinking.'

'This is not a game. It's how Panther, Rabbit and me live. The stuff I steal Panther sells. That's how we survive.'

Oriole put her head to one side. 'Mellow taught me that it is wrong to take something that does not belong to you.'

'If you can get away with it then it's okay. That's what Panther says.'

'Well, that Panther is wrong,' Oriole said, firmly.

'No, he's not. He's very smart.' Boy turned his head away and frowned. This girl who he had just saved from death had no right to tell him what was right and what was wrong. 'You don't know what it's like living in Soulless,' he said. 'It's mean and hard. If you want to survive you have to be mean and hard too.'

Boy's voice suddenly sounded cold and this worried Oriole. 'I am sorry, Boy,' she said, touching his arm. 'I do not know what it is like to live in a city, especially one like Solace, where people never smile. In my Forest I dig for roots or pick fruit from the trees. I do not need money. I do not need to light-finger. Please, let us not speak of it any more. It makes me hurt inside.'

'It hurts me inside too,' he said, turning to face her again. 'Do you want to see my treasure?' He rummaged up his sleeve, took out the silver box and opened it.

'Why, this is a feather, Boy,' Oriole said, excitedly, holding up the turquoise blue treasure. 'Where did you get it?'

'I found it when I was light-fingering the other day.'

Oriole suddenly lifted her head. 'What was that?' she said, as a mournful groaning sound came from above.

'It's the city walls. They make funny noises when the wind blows a certain way.'

'They sound so sad,' said Oriole, 'like the dying breath of an old tree before it falls.' She clutched the ragged blanket Boy had put about her shoulders. 'I do not want to be sad so I will give you a song, Boy. Close your eyes now and open your heart.'

Oriole opened her mouth and the most beautiful sound Boy had ever heard poured out of her. *So this was singing!*

He closed his eyes and listened, and as he listened a

forest grew in his own mind, tree by tree, until it spread to fill every space. In and out of the branches birds of every colour fluttered about. He saw morning mist lying in a thin sheet above the ground and a sky smudged with pink and orange clouds. As the notes ascended, Boy floated up to the tallest and oldest tree in the forest, where he sat in a nest held fast in its branches. From there he could see the wide stretch of plain all the way to the purple mountains beyond. Boy sat there, entranced.

When Oriole's song was over, he opened his eyes and stared at her silently.

'What is the matter?' she asked. 'Did you not like my song?'

'No, it was beautiful. It was as if I was dreaming but awake.' Then he tilted his head. 'But I have heard something like it before, Oriole.'

Boy squeezed his eyes tight, trying to remember. Then he suddenly opened them. 'It was in the Demon Monster's mansion! And I remember something else, too. The man I stole this feather from had a hook scar on his face. He and the Demon Monster are the same person!'

'A song, a feather and a hook scar. These are all signs, Boy,' Oriole said excitedly. 'Tomorrow you will take me to the Demon Monster's nest.'

13

THE LADY BUTTERFLY

Boy did not tell Oriole about the Demon Monster's reputation for eating children, nor did he mention the moving statues in the garden. Instead, hiding his fear behind a brave face – for had she not called him *brave* and *strong*? – he led Oriole across the city to the market place and to the small hole in the wall.

He kept a careful watch for Panther in the weak dawn light, for he knew he would be hunting him down. Boy had never stayed away this long before. But he would never go back, not now. Oriole had shown him a different path and he knew it was the right one to follow. Even if it meant leaving his treasures behind, she had given him so much more – hope, song, long-forgotten memories and love. And he still had his most precious find – the turquoise feather in the silver box.

Parting the weeds, Boy crawled through first and then called to Oriole to follow.

'It is a forest!' she cried with delight when she stood up on the other side of the wall. She smiled as she looked around, but her smile soon faded.

This forest was different. In the Forest of Birds the trees chatted when the sun came up and murmured as it went down. In the Demon Monster's garden the trees stood silent.

'Even the trees are sad in the City of Solace, Boy,' she sighed. 'That is because there are so many walls to block them in. Walls inside walls inside more walls . . .'

'There has to be walls,' said Boy. 'Nobody would know where they belonged or what belonged to them and everything would be a mess.'

'There are no walls in my Forest. Yet everything that lives in it knows its right place.'

Boy shivered. 'Sounds a bit scary. You know, Oriole, you're saying the name of the city wrong. It's Soulless not Solace.'

'I am calling it by its old name. I like it much better, don't you?'

Boy didn't know what *solace* meant, but he didn't want to let Oriole know that, so he just shrugged his shoulders.

'Solace is when you are sad or in distress and someone comes to comfort you,' said Oriole, as if reading his thoughts.

'That *is* a much better name,' Boy agreed. 'Come on. The Demon Monster's mansion is this way.'

Boy led Oriole along a path littered with leaves and small twigs that snaked through the trees. He couldn't help but notice how loud his own footsteps were compared to hers. She was behind him and yet he couldn't hear or feel her presence at all. It was as if she was a shadow or one of those creatures with wings . . . what did she call them? Birds. Yes, a small bird flying with her feet not touching the ground.

There were fruit trees. Boy could see them clearly now that it was daylight. Oranges hung like round lanterns from the branches. And red apples, too, some the size of small melons. In all his travels through the City of Soulless, Boy had never once seen a fruit tree. All the fruit sold in the market was brought in by the travelling merchants.

Soon they came to the clearing. Oriole clasped her hands to her chest when she saw the statues. She ran to the middle of them, first turning to face the giant tortoise, then the tiger sharpening his claws on a tree, then the dragon. And lastly she turned to the many-limbed beast. Her face grew pale.

'Careful, Oriole,' Boy said, standing back at the edge of the clearing.

'Who turned this bird into stone?' Oriole's voice was strangely unmusical as she touched one of the wings. 'Was it the Demon Monster?' She felt a darkness grow inside her and her skin begin to prickle. It was a new feeling that she did not like at all.

'They aren't real; they're statues,' Boy said, although he still wasn't sure himself. 'A stonemason carved them out of rock.'

Oriole sighed. 'There are so many things I need to learn about the Outside.' She began climbing the statue, stepping on one wing to get higher and higher until she was sitting astride the creature's neck. 'Is he not magnificent, Boy?'

Boy nodded, though he was still watching for that glint of life in the creature's eye. He was relieved when Oriole climbed down and walked on ahead.

The Demon Monster's mansion at night had appeared small and dark and threatening. In the daylight, Boy could see that it was a two-storey building made from stone and honey-coloured wood. There were five lattice windows covered with rice paper that ran along the top floor and a verandah stretched across the front.

They walked quietly up to the house.

'How do we get into his nest?' Oriole whispered, pushing on one of the windows. Her finger accidentally broke through the rice paper and she put her eye to it.

'What do you see?' Boy asked at her shoulder.

'A fire, table, chairs. But no Demon Monster,' she replied. 'I am going to knock on the door.'

Boy kept close to Oriole in case she needed protection. There was the scrape of a chair and footsteps approaching the door. And then it slid open.

Oriole looked up in surprise. Standing before them was a beautiful lady in a dress of apple-green silk with a pink-and-blue border of embroidered butterflies. Over the dress she wore a vest with a collar of white fur. Her face was a perfect oval with brown eyes that sparkled and her hair was swept up into a swirling knot and fastened with a gold pin, a tiny filigree bird dangling off the end.

Oriole was so taken by the woman's beauty that she could not utter a sound. At last she said, 'My name is Oriole and this is Boy. We were wondering if the Demon Monster was in his nest.'

The lady visibly started.

'She means: Is Uncle at home?' Boy said sheepishly.

The lady tilted her head at Oriole and smiled, which made the tiny filigree bird dance and twirl.

'Wait here,' she said, then turned with a giggle and

walked into the mansion.

'You mustn't call him Demon Monster,' Boy said.

'Why not?'

'Because it's rude.'

Oriole was confused. 'But that is what you call him.'

'We don't know his real name so we've always called him Demon Monster,' said Boy. 'Call him Uncle, that's the polite way, all right? Shh . . . she's coming back.'

The Demon Monster appeared at the door with the beautiful lady beside him.

'She sings, Uncle . . . like a little bird. She is the one. Say something, Oriole dear. Say something so my uncle can hear.'

Boy couldn't understand what was happening. He looked at the Demon Monster, then at the lady, then at Oriole. It was almost as if they all knew each other.

'Uncle,' Oriole began in her lovely musical voice, 'I came to the City of Solace to find a way to save the King and thereby cure our Mellow.'

As Oriole spoke, the old man unknitted his brow and the scar on his cheek turned into a circle as he smiled.

'My dear,' he said with affection, 'we have been waiting for you for a very long time.'

14
THE PRINCE AND THE NIGHTINGALE

How strange the people of the Outside are, Oriole thought, looking up at the Demon Monster. *Some are sunny and clever like Boy, who is still so young. Some are dark and full of poison like the Lord Chancellor, who is supposed to serve the King but only serves himself. And some are old and very wise but are called Demon Monsters.*

'Come, Oriole. I am Lady Butterfly,' said the beautiful lady, ushering her inside. 'I will make some refreshments. Children are always hungry, are they not? I have no children of my own, but every time I see a child there is food in their little hands.' She turned with a swish of green and pink silk.

Oriole followed Lady Butterfly and the Demon Monster into the house. When she could not feel Boy behind her she looked over her shoulder. He was hanging about the door, hands in his pockets, head bowed.

'Come, Boy,' she beckoned. 'What is the matter with you?'

Boy shook his head. 'Lady Butterfly didn't invite me,' he whispered. 'I'll wait for you in the market square.'

'Are you two children coming or not?' Lady Butterfly suddenly appeared behind Oriole.

'Yes, we are coming.' Oriole smiled at Boy. She grabbed his hand and pulled him inside.

A plate of crisp, flaky pastries filled with lotus-nut paste was placed on the table. Then hot spring-onion pancakes sprinkled with salt. And after that, Lady Butterfly served up a bowl of sweet walnut soup infused with scented cassia flowers.

Boy was a common thief who had lived off the pickings of others for most of his life. He had never eaten such delicacies before. He bit into a small bun and licked the sesame seeds off his fingers. The porcelain bowls and plates the food was served on were so fine he could almost see through them. *Each one of these must be worth a lot of money,* he thought. *It would be easy to slip one under my vest to take back to Panther.* But then he looked at Oriole and the thought slipped away as quickly as it had come.

'Eat up. There is more,' Lady Butterfly said.

Oriole ate with small delicate bites. Every so often she glanced up at the Demon Monster. He had a kind face, and she wondered why everyone was afraid of him. He sipped tea silently, occasionally spitting out the long green leaves onto the table. Oriole was longing to ask him about the King and Mellow. He seemed such a wise man – surely he would know what to do. But his eyes were looking inwards like Mellow's did when he was thinking, and she knew to leave him be.

After Lady Butterfly had cleared away the dishes, the Demon Monster finally spoke. 'My name is Lord Taku and I would like to tell you a story,' he said.

Lady Butterfly sat down beside him, hands resting in her lap, her head tilted. A soft wind blew through the lattice window, making the fire in the hearth dance. The room grew so quiet that Oriole saw a little grey mouse peep out of a hole in the floorboards, thinking everyone had gone to bed.

'For the past thousand years there has been a succession of Kings who looked after the Kingdom of Pafir and its city,' he began. 'Each King was wise and strong and loved by his people. And the Kingdom flourished.'

Lord Taku paused and Lady Butterfly refilled his cup from a little clay teapot shaped like a lotus flower.

'The King who rules us today was also once kind and

wise,' Lord Taku continued, 'but he was also weak. After he married he had a son who was an adventurous boy. The Queen died when the boy was young, and the King was devastated. So he lavished all his love upon his only child. The young prince would go riding in the forests that surrounded the City of Solace to hunt wild animals – deer, boar and birds – with his bow and arrow.'

Oriole did not like to hear about hunting. She put her hand up to her throat.

'One day the young prince heard about a forest far away at the borders where the Kingdom of Pafir meets the neighbouring Kingdom of Nanor. It was said that the Forest was filled with rare and exotic birds whose feathers dazzled the eye. *What a sight to see,* he thought. *How pleased my father would be if I returned with some of these beautiful creatures.* And so, telling no one but his manservant who he took with him, and with his bow and arrows across his back and a dagger at his belt, the Prince quietly rode through the Western Gate.

'They travelled for days along tracks barely visible until finally they reached the edge of a mighty forest. The chatter of birds excited the Prince after his long journey. He looked up and saw creatures of such vivid colours and of such strange design he was amazed. Some had long trailing tails, others wore feathery crowns on their heads.

'As nightfall was fast approaching, they set up a temporary shelter. The Prince took off his bow and arrows and removed his belt and dagger and laid them beside him on the ground. Now, this dagger was a highly prized weapon. It had been in the royal family for hundreds of years and the King had presented it to the Prince on his eighteenth birthday only the week before. It was made of jade from the Kunlun Mountains and could cut through any metal with ease. But what was even more valuable were the precious stones embedded in its hilt. One jewel was an emerald, the other a ruby. Legend had it that if someone with the Sight looked into the stones they would see into the future, see the truth. However, in all the dagger's long existence, only a handful of people had this ability, and neither the Prince nor the King did.'

Boy sat up tall in his seat as he imagined himself, a Prince sitting on a white horse with the magical dagger at his waist.

'The next morning when the Prince awoke, he reached for his weapons. But they were not there. He turned to his manservant, who was feeding the horses, and asked if he had taken them.

'"No, my Prince," the manservant replied.

'The Prince stood up angrily. "Someone else is in this forest. Quickly, saddle my horse."

'A short distance away from the camp, he found the precious dagger, then the bow and arrows. But every arrow had been snapped in two. Then, as he was returning to his camp, there came a beautiful song. So pure and clear was the sound the Prince was entranced. He felt immense joy as he thought how he would capture the bird and take it as a gift back to the King.

'The Prince dismounted and beckoned to his manservant to circle one way while he circled the other. The song started again. The prince followed it. But it was as elusive as mist – first calling from the treetops and then from the undergrowth. After a day's searching, the Prince and his manservant gave up as darkness was fast approaching. The manservant lit a fire and he and the Prince spent another night in the forest.

'When he awoke the next morning the Prince found a brilliant turquoise feather lying beside him. As he turned it in his fingers it shimmered gold, then silver, then deep blue. *Had the strange songbird dropped this feather?* he wondered. *Had it stood over him during the night and watched him sleep?*

'He decided to set a trap and made a lasso out of twine, which he laid in a circle on the ground. Breaking off some of the sweet bun they had eaten for breakfast, he placed it inside the lasso. Then with one end of the rope in his

hand, the Prince hid behind a tree and waited. He waited all day and finally he heard the glorious song again. It drew closer and closer. The Prince's eyes were wide with excitement and his fingers twitched against the rope. The ferns shuddered, then they parted. But walking towards him was not a bird at all, but a beautiful girl.'

15

THE FORESTS BURNED

'A girl?' Oriole whispered. Tears clouded her vision. 'A girl who sang like a bird?'

Lord Taku's eyes fell on Oriole and he nodded gently. 'She was sixteen years old with long dark hair and brilliant green eyes. She wore a dress of golden thread that shimmered as she moved.'

Oriole touched her own dress without thinking.

'The Prince watched the girl, hardly daring to breathe. The girl tiptoed forward, looking at the bun the Prince had left in the lasso. Then she stepped inside the rope.'

'And did he get her?' Boy asked.

'The manservant nudged the Prince to draw tight the rope, but the Prince did not move.'

'Why?' Boy said. 'Didn't he want to catch her?'

'Yes,' Lord Taku replied. 'But the Prince had fallen in love. When the girl saw the Prince hiding behind the tree she turned to flee.

'"Wait," the Prince called out in the gentlest voice he could. He did not want to frighten her. "Please, do not go."

'To his surprise the girl stopped and turned back slowly. She was not afraid of the Prince even though he was a hunter and had brought weapons to her forest.'

'Why was she not scared of him?' asked Oriole.

'In the night she had gazed upon him while he slept. And do you know what had happened?' Lord Taku smiled.

Oriole and Boy shook their heads.

'She had also fallen in love. With the Prince.'

Lord Taku rested his arms on the table and leaned forward. He took a sip of tea and put the cup down gently. 'The Prince sent his manservant home to tell the King that he had fallen in love and that he would not be returning to the Palace.

'"Who is this girl?" the King demanded of the manservant. "Is she of royal blood?"

'"No, Your High One," the servant replied. "She is a girl who lives alone in the forest and sings like a bird."'

Oriole touched her fingers to her lips.

'The King turned to his Wishbird. Mellow had been sitting perched on the arm of the throne, listening quietly the whole time.

'"What do I do, Mellow?" the King asked. He and the Wishbird were very close and he trusted Mellow completely. "How will I bring my son back?"

'"You must not use force," Mellow said. "That will only drive the Prince further away. Welcome this bird girl into the Palace."

'But the King was angry and this time he did not listen to his Wishbird's advice. He ordered ten soldiers to go and capture the Prince and bring him home.'

'Did they find him?' Oriole asked.

Lord Taku shook his head. 'The King, in desperation, then asked for my advice.'

'You?' Boy said confused.

'I was Lord Chancellor in those days,' he replied.

Oriole and Boy looked at each other in shock.

'"Agree to their marriage," I told him. "That is the only way." But he sent his soldiers out again to try and bring the Prince back by force, for he believed that his son had been bewitched by the girl who sang like a bird.

'Three more weeks passed. The soldiers once again returned empty-handed.' Lord Taku let out a long sigh. 'What happened next was a terrible tragedy. The King was so angered by this news that he bellowed, "Cut down the forests. Burn them out!"'

Oriole's heart cried in pain.

'Months turned into years as forest after forest was burned. A terrible sickness had come over the King. He was heartbroken and angry and turned on his city in despair. Any song or laughter reminded him of his son. So he ordered music be banned and all musicians be taken away in carts he had especially built. They came to be known by the people as the Song Stealer's Carts.'

Boy sat up when he heard this, but he did not speak. He was watching Oriole, whose eyes glistened with tears.

'Moreover, the King had every bird in the city killed. He told the townspeople to bang pots and pans so that the birds could not land, and when the poor creatures fell to the ground they were beaten to death with sticks and stones. Then he banished his Wishbird from the Kingdom.'

Oriole hid her face in her hands. Tears stained her dress of spider's silk. Lady Butterfly stood up and went to sit beside her. She took Oriole's small trembling hand in hers and held it to her.

'But unbeknownst to the King, a baby was born to the couple. The Wishbird himself promised to look after her and hid her safely away in the Forest of Birds.

'What happened to them, Lord Taku?' Oriole finally whispered. 'What happened to my parents?'

'They were killed when the forests burned.'

16

IT BELONGS TO
HER NOW

It took a moment for the words to sink in. Then Boy
stared at Oriole. 'You mean the Prince is your father?
Which means the King . . . ' Boy gulped. 'You are a
princess, Oriole,' he said in awe.

Mellow had been both mother and father to Oriole.
Now she realised why he had never told her about
them. If she had known of her parents' death and her
relationship to the King then she would never have felt
she fully belonged in the Forest of Birds; she would have
always been haunted by the Outside. He knew that should
she ever set foot in the City of Solace, the King, her own
grandfather, would have her put to death.

Lady Butterfly squeezed Oriole's hand and went to
make more tea and cut up some oranges and apples.

No one spoke for a very long while.

Then Boy said, 'I have a question, Lord Taku.' The sweet juice of an orange dribbled down his chin. He wiped it with his sleeve. 'It seemed you knew that Oriole was coming, but how could you?'

'It is written in a prophecy,' said Lord Taku. *'"In a time of great despair, a person of royal blood will deliver the Kingdom from its troubles."'*

He looked at Oriole.

'But I do not have the power to make a dying King well or stop a Barbarian Army from invading,' said Oriole. 'Please tell me what I should do.'

Lord Taku stood. His body was bent, like an old tree heavy with snow. 'I am sorry, child, but I do not have an answer for you.'

'But Mellow will die, Lord Taku. I have to find a way.'

'It saddens me that Mellow is so unwell, just as it saddens me that the King is ailing . . .' Lord Taku swayed on his feet.

Lady Butterfly rose from her chair and went to him. 'Children, Uncle is very tired. It is time for you to go.' She gently escorted Lord Taku to a chair by the fire and covered his lap with a blanket.

'Butterfly,' he said, and pointed to the wall where there was a small cupboard. 'It is time to give it to her.'

The sky outside had misted over and Oriole heard drops of rain on the roof.

Lady Butterfly looked at Lord Taku and a small frown appeared. 'Uncle, are you sure? She is still so young.'

'It belongs to her now,' he replied.

Lady Butterfly took a brass key from a drawer and unlocked the cupboard door. She looked back at her uncle once, twice, as if giving him a chance to change his mind.

'Everything will be all right, Butterfly,' Lord Taku nodded. 'She has wisdom. Mellow has taught her well . . .'

Lady Butterfly drew out something wrapped in orange brocade. Carrying it carefully, she set it down in front of Lord Taku.

'Come, Oriole,' Lord Taku said.

Oriole hesitated, strangely fearful, then straightened her shoulders and went to stand by his side. She looked at the wrapped object and gasped. She knew what lay beneath.

'What is it?' Boy asked.

'My father's dagger,' she said as the cloth fell away.

The dagger was encased in a gold filigree sheath and it was exquisite. Oriole knew that daggers were used for killing and yet she could not help but admire its beauty – the two precious stones, the emerald and the ruby, seemed to glow against the pale jade blade.

'Take great care of it, Oriole,' Lord Taku said. 'And guard it well. There are many who covet such a treasure. Maybe you have the Sight. Maybe you will see the truth in the stones and they will show you a way to save the Kingdom of Pafir and Mellow.'

'I do not understand. Why do you have the dagger?' Oriole asked.

'When your father's manservant returned from the forest, he brought the jade dagger with him. The Prince no longer felt the passion to hunt or kill. But the manservant also brought back something else even more precious.'

'What was that?' she asked.

'A feather, a turquoise blue feather that came from your mother, Nightingale,' Lord Taku replied. 'I used to keep it in a silver box close to me always. But one day, when I was out in the streets, it was stolen.'

Boy's mouth fell open and he flushed with heat. He stared down at his fingers. How could he tell Lord Taku that he was the one who had stolen it? He would be sent from the house immediately. Oriole would hate him.

'My mother's feather?' Oriole said.

'Yes,' Lord Taku replied looking at Boy, knowingly.

There was a long silence that stretched across the room.

Boy didn't dare raise his eyes as he put his hand up his sleeve and brought out the silver box. It didn't belong to him. As much as he loved it, he knew he couldn't keep it. 'It was me who stole it,' he said in a small whisper, and placed the box on the table. 'I'm sorry, Lord Taku.'

'Now our trust in you is complete, Boy,' Lord Taku said, gently, and he nudged the box over to Oriole. 'It is yours now, my child.'

Boy flushed as Oriole smiled at him and picked up the silver box reverently – it wasn't the reaction he had expected and he felt a glow deep inside.

'Come, children,' Lady Butterfly said.

As they walked through the garden to the hole in the wall, Boy stopped. 'Lady Butterfly,' he said. 'Have you heard of the Golden Note Studio?'

'Why, of course. Master Rui and Madame Naa were two of the finest musicians in the city.'

'They were my parents,' he said.

Lady Butterfly looked at him sadly. 'You must have great skill in those fingers, Boy.'

Boy reddened. He did not want her to know how he used that skill. 'Are they still alive?'

'My uncle has tried in vain to find out what happened to all the musicians, for many were his friends, including your parents. Lord Taku is a wonderful musician himself and taught me how to sing,' Lady Butterfly said.

'So it *was* you I heard the first time I came to your house,' Boy said. 'Why weren't you and Lord Taku taken away too?'

'My uncle and the King were childhood friends and used to play together in the Palace grounds. When the King ordered that all music be outlawed, he told Lord Taku to go into hiding, to stay in his house and not show his face in the city again. And he told me to take care of my uncle. We then built a wall around this house and garden . . .'

'And made up the rumours about the Demon Monster and eating children?' Boy said.

Lady Butterfly laughed. 'We had to stop people from coming here.' Then she grew sad again, her eyes distant. 'Over time we watched the people forget that music once filled their streets. They do not even remember what a song is any longer. They have forgotten, too, that forests filled with birds once surrounded the city.' She sighed. 'Now the city is called Soulless. Few remember its real name. Without music, a city loses its soul and people's hearts begin to die. That is what has happened to the King.'

'And that is why Mellow is so ill,' Oriole said.

Lady Butterfly touched the dagger in Oriole's hand. 'Look for the truth in the stones, Oriole.'

Late that night, as pale clouds drifted across the sky, Oriole and Boy squeezed into the hideaway in Burnt Water Alley. A rat scurried by. When it saw the two children it squeaked with fright and ran away.

'The creatures of the city are all so frightened,' said Oriole.

'Rats are disgusting things,' Boy said, wrinkling his nose.

'Not to me. How I miss the soft hooting of night birds and seeing the sky fill with stars.'

'I would like to go to your Forest of Birds one day, Oriole.'

'And so you shall. I will take you there when . . .

when I have saved Mellow.'

'And saved the City of Soulless,' Boy added.

Oriole picked up the jade dagger. She held it to the candle flame and stared into the emerald, moving it at different angles.

'See anything?' Boy asked.

'Only my own reflection.'

'Try the ruby.'

Oriole put the ruby up to one eye and stared deep into the heart of it.

'Anything?'

She shook her head.

'You are tired,' Boy said. He took the dagger from Oriole's hand and she let him, then he laid it beside him on the ground and placed a tattered blanket over them both.

18
MELLOW

As Mellow lay dying, he remembered the day when he fled the Palace, taking with him as many birds as he could. They flew through days and nights. And they had to fly high, for below them the forests burned. Smoke filled the air, blotting out the sun. Many birds fell from exhaustion. They were too small and their tiny hearts were not strong enough. When Mellow found the forest where the Prince was hiding, the soldiers had arrived too. The sound of wood crackling and the roar of flames was terrifying.

Mellow could sense the Prince. He had the familiar smell of the Palace still on him. He was by a stream and a girl sat beside him holding a baby wrapped in a feather blanket. They did not speak but looked lovingly down at the infant.

'Mellow,' cried the Prince, when he saw the Wishbird. 'You have come. This is my beloved Nightingale.' He placed an arm around the girl.

Mellow greeted Nightingale, but when she replied it was in a beautiful song Mellow had never heard before and did not understand.

'Where does she come from?' Mellow asked.

'I do not know,' the Prince replied. 'But sometimes her arms become wings and feathers appear on her skin.' The Prince stroked the girl's long hair. 'Perhaps one day she will be able to tell me.' Then his face grew serious. 'But we do not have much time, Mellow,' he said, looking at the smoke drifting towards them. 'You must take our baby, take her far away where my father will not find her. You must keep her safe.'

'Where will you go?' Mellow asked.

'We will lead the soldiers away. Our daughter is called Oriole. Teach her the ways of goodness and love. And please, Mellow, promise never to tell her about us or the King. She must never go to the City of Solace or he will destroy her.'

Mellow knew there was no other way. 'I understand,' he said. He watched the couple kiss their child one last time, and then the Prince took Nightingale's hand and they ran away together through the forest.

Mellow flew to the highest tree. He summoned the birds, who came at once. They carried the baby far away to a forest where an ancient Banyan tree grew. And there in its giant branches the child was raised. And Mellow kept his promise and never told her about her parents.

But now Oriole was in grave danger. Mellow knew from the rumour of small things on the land and in the sky that the Barbarian Army was drawing close to the City of Solace.

19

THE BETRAYAL

Rabbit was looking for a stall that sold a delicious kind of mushroom. It was late, almost dusk, and it was his last errand before going back to the shack and to Panther.

He was about to buy the mushrooms from the vendor when he saw Boy in the distance. He hadn't seen Boy since he had left for the Demon Monster's mansion. Rabbit thought that Boy must have met a terrible fate and he had been sick with grief. He'd kept looking over at Boy's unrumpled bedding, hoping that he would suddenly appear. But now, here Boy was, safe and whole, thanks to the wing-footed God of Honourable Thieves.

Rabbit was about to call out when he saw that Boy was not alone. There was a girl with him, a strange-looking girl. She had long shining dark hair, odd shoes that looked like they were woven from vines, and a dress made of a type of cloth Rabbit had never seen before.

Rabbit watched as they slipped between two buildings. He ran up to the narrow passageway and peeped in. He could see their shadows. Then they seemed to disappear.

Pulling at his earlobe, Rabbit wondered why Boy hadn't come home. He thought long and hard about what to do next. *Boy needs Panther to protect him from the bad gangs,* he told himself. *He's just a kid. And he needs me to cook for him – how skinny and pale he looks.*

He was about to go after Boy when he stopped. Another thought had struck him. *Maybe Boy had actually stolen a treasure from the Demon Monster and the girl is trying to trick him out of it? What if she's leading him right now to her gang's hideout? No, the best thing to do is to tell Panther. He will know what to do.*

So Rabbit turned and scurried back to the shack at the end of Ratskin Alley.

In the middle of the night, Boy awoke. Something had disturbed him from his sleep. He looked at Oriole. The moon shining down into the tiny alcove caught her cheek so it glowed silvery white. Boy's thoughts turned to the precious dagger. Earlier in the night, Oriole had looked into the stones, first the emerald then the ruby, but had seen nothing. Boy was longing to try, but he was too embarrassed to ask. *What if I have the Sight?* he kept thinking. *The stones might tell me where my ana and ata are.*

He reached down beside him, feeling for the dagger. It was not where he had left it. Carefully, so as not to wake Oriole, he searched the alcove. Then he felt something small, hard and circular stuck into the fibres of the blanket. He prised it out. It was an earring.

'Panther,' he whispered in horror. *He's been here, and he's stolen the dagger.*

Boy groaned silently. He had made up his mind never to go back to Panther. Now he had no choice. He had to get the dagger back or the city would be lost and Mellow would die. And Boy would never know about his ana and ata.

He looked down at Oriole sleeping, stroked her hair gently, then crawled out of the alcove. As he made his way to Ratskin Alley, he thought long and hard about his plan.

When Boy opened the door of the shack, Panther pounced. 'If you've come for the dagger, forget it,' he hissed. 'You were meant to share your find with us but you kept it for yourself.'

'Dagger?' Boy replied. 'That's the least of the treasures at the Demon Monster's mansion. There's a lot more stuff. I just need your help to get it.'

'You hungry, Boy?' Rabbit said, overjoyed to see Boy safe. 'I can cook you some –'

'Forget food for once, Rabbit!' Panther snapped. 'There's more important business to attend to.' He cocked his head to one side, a greedy look on his face as he turned to Boy again. 'More treasure, you say?'

'Yes, so much I need help to carry it. And easy to get at, too. Come and I'll show you, Panther.'

Panther moved uneasily, a twitch in his right cheek. He went to twirl the earring in his earlobe and was surprised to find it gone.

'Is this what you're looking for?' Boy said, holding up the small silver ring as if it were a trophy.

Panther grabbed the earring from Boy and put it back through his ear. 'What about the Demon Monster? Is he . . . er . . . dangerous?'

Boy realised that Panther was afraid. The thought made him feel grown-up.

'The Demon Monster is terrifying, murderous and cunning,' he said. 'But I think he'll be asleep. You just follow me and we should be safe.'

Panther hesitated. A look crossed his face that was both scared and greedy. Finally, he nodded. 'All right then. Bring me the looting bag, Rabbit.'

'Rabbit better stay here,' Boy said. 'You know how clumsy he can be. We don't want to wake the Demon Monster.'

Rabbit looked hurt, but Boy knew that deep inside he was glad to stay behind.

'Looks like we've finally found the big prize,' Panther said, trying to cover his nervousness. He put on his jacket, thrust the jade dagger into his waistband, and followed Boy.

When they got to the wall, Panther had trouble wriggling through the hole. He was much bigger than Boy. The vines tugged and tore his clothes, and by the time he came out the other side he was in a foul temper.

'So where is this treasure room?' he demanded.

'Just a little further,' Boy said. He led Panther deep into the trees. Even though it was dark, he knew the way by heart now. Behind him, he could hear Panther stumbling over roots and running into low branches.

'Lucky that Demon Monster is asleep,' murmured Panther.

It took a few moments for Panther to realise that Boy

had disappeared. He stopped and looked around.

'Boy!' he whispered. 'Where are you?'

There was no reply. When he was following Boy, Panther had been thinking about all the treasures they were going to steal and how rich they were going to be. But now fear set in stronger than before. He was lost amongst these strange tall trees, in a place like he had never imagined.

'Panther,' he heard Boy whisper. 'Over here.'

He stumbled towards the voice.

Then Boy said, 'Don't move!'

Panther stopped and looked up. Huge shapes loomed over him in the dark. His first thought was that it was the Demon Monster himself. He didn't dare breathe. He wanted to call out to Boy. Where was he?

Then the clouds broke apart and moonlight flooded the garden. There, above him, was an enormous creature! And Boy was riding the shoulders of this beast!

Panther cried out in terror.

'Take out the dagger and put it on the ground,' Boy said fiercely. 'These are the beasts of the Demon Monster. They are the reason people disappear in here. But I have become their friend.' He patted the creature he was riding. 'Put down the dagger and I will stop them from eating you. But be quick – I cannot hold them for long.'

Panther glanced around in fear. Other terrible creatures surrounded him. He was trapped. He stared up at Boy. Slowly, reaching behind him, he pulled out the dagger and dropped it on the ground.

Boy slid down off the statue, walked over to Panther, and picked up the dagger. 'Thank you, Panther. This dagger will save the city. We had to have it back.'

'Who's we? And why are these beasts just standing there?' Panther was starting to realise that he had been tricked. He scowled. 'Why you little . . .'

He lunged at Boy. A noose slipped over his neck from behind and tightened, pulling him back.

· 'Sorry, Panther,' Boy said. 'Meet the Demon Monster. You'll be staying at his house for a little while.'

Behind Panther, Lord Taku grinned at Boy and nodded. Boy gave him a little bow of respect, then ran back through the forest to the hole in the wall.

20
A NEW KIND OF LIGHT

Oriole woke with a start. Boy was gone. She waited, listening carefully for his footsteps. Then she began to worry. Maybe he had left her and gone back to his old life. She wrapped the ragged blanket around her shoulders and thought about Mellow, wondering how he was.

It was not quite dawn when she heard someone approaching. It was Boy's soft tread. She peeped out and, relieved, saw him sidling up the narrow passage.

'I was so worried. Where did you go?' she asked.

Boy pulled out the dagger and sat down beside Oriole. 'Panther stole it when we were sleeping. So I got it back.' Then he told Oriole of how he had lured Panther into the Demon Monster's garden.

'You should have seen Panther's face when he saw me riding the bird creature,' Boy laughed. 'And now the Demon Monster has him tied up inside his house.'

'How very brave and clever you are, Boy,' Oriole said, touching his arm.

Boy's chest swelled with pride. Then he yawned, feeling suddenly very tired. 'Now that Panther knows where we are, we have to find another hideaway. I'll just rest for a bit first.'

He put his head on his knees and was fast asleep in moments.

As Oriole watched Boy sleep, she felt a heaviness in her chest. How could someone so small and alone be so brave? He had rescued her from the dungeon and helped her find her precious dagger. Underneath all the bluff and talk, he was good and kind. Yet he had no one – no home, no family. At least she had Mellow and the birds and her Forest. Her heart ached for him.

Suddenly Oriole heard the sound of someone big squeezing down the passageway. She prodded Boy urgently in the ribs.

'What is it?' he asked, groggily.

'Someone is coming,' Oriole whispered.

The puffing and panting grew closer, and the person cursed under his breath.

Boy sat up in alarm. 'It's Panther! He must have escaped Lord Taku. We have to get out of here, now.'

Suddenly a large hand reached into the alcove.

Oriole cried out and pushed herself as far back as she could go to avoid the grabbing hand. Something rushed through her, but how strange she felt. It was as if a tree root was twisting and coiling inside her stomach. Blood was rushing through her veins, into her arms and along her back, and there was an intense itching sensation all over her body.

Boy quickly unsheathed the dagger and stabbed Panther's hand once, twice.

Panther withdrew his hand, screaming in pain.

'Run, Oriole!' Boy cried, and they scrambled in the opposite direction down the narrow passageway.

Oriole found it hard to go fast. Something was wrong. Her stomach felt hard and her skin . . . if only she could stop the unbearable itching. She could hear that Panther boy breathing and grunting loudly not far behind them, and she forced herself to keep going.

Finally, they fell out into a laneway and raced off through the night like animals fleeing a ferocious fire.

When they came to a junction where two alleys crossed, Boy hesitated. 'This way,' he finally said and pulled on Oriole's arm.

But this time he had made the wrong decision. A two-storey building blocked their escape.

'Oriole,' Boy said as they turned. 'Stay behind me.'

Panther stood there, grinning at them. 'That wasn't very smart, was it, little rat?' he said. 'You tricked me once and you're not going to do it again.'

'Don't come any closer,' Boy said, raising the dagger.

'How big and brave you are in front of your friend. Why don't you tell her how you cry like a baby when I beat you. How you snivel and grovel and beg for mercy. You're just a worthless little cockroach and now I'm going to squash you.'

As Panther spoke, the roots inside Oriole's stomach grew tighter and tighter, twisting around themselves until she had to cry out. 'Stop! Leave him be!'

The notes were so piercing they tore through Boy's body and he had to cover his ears with his hands.

Panther stared at Oriole. 'Hey, you're the girl with the singing tongue. Well, well. The Lord Chancellor has offered a large reward for your return, you know.'

A new feeling came over Oriole. Her skin no longer itched. It felt cool, as if she had been sprayed with a fine mist. She looked down in surprise at the turquoise feathers erupting from her arms. They were small at first, but very quickly they lengthened and spread across her shoulders and down her back.

Panther gasped and stepped backwards.

'What is happening to me?' Oriole said. Soon her arms had disappeared and in their place was a set of magnificent turquoise wings.

Boy stared in wonderment. She was beautiful.

'Step behind me, place your arms around my neck and hold on tightly,' Oriole whispered.

And as Panther charged at them, she lifted her wings and they flew.

21

BIRD GIRL

Oriole and Boy stood on the roof of the two-storey building that blocked the alley. They looked down at Panther, who was prowling back and forth.

'I flew like a bird,' Oriole said, smiling. She looked at her wings, long and full and soft by her sides. She lifted one up. Even though it was bigger and longer than her arm, it felt so much lighter.

'You carried me up here as if I was a bit of dust. You were so strong,' Boy said, staring at her.

Oriole nodded. 'It is all so new and strange. It seemed to happen when that Panther boy was saying horrible things to you.'

'You were angry.'

'Is that what that feeling is called?'

'Yes, but usually it doesn't change people into birds,' laughed Boy. 'We are not safe here. Panther is more dangerous than ever now that he knows what you can do. We need to find a place to hide.'

'Then we will wait for that Panther to leave and then go to Lord Taku's mansion,' Oriole said. 'He will not dare to go there again.'

By the time they arrived in the walled garden, Oriole's wings and feathers had disappeared.

'You are truly your mother's child,' Lady Butterfly said as she sat them down with some sweet walnut tea and they told her of their adventures.

Lord Taku's face grew grave. 'This is bad,' he said. 'I am sorry Panther escaped. Now he knows of your powers, Oriole.'

'But they will both be safe here, won't they, Uncle?' Lady Butterfly asked.

'For the moment, yes,' Lord Taku replied. Then he sighed and stood up, looking out the window. 'Very soon, though, we will all be in danger.'

'How so, Uncle?'

'The Barbarian Army will be upon us any day,' replied Lord Taku, closing the shutter.

'The Lord Chancellor is a traitor,' Boy said. 'Oriole heard him send a messenger to the leader of the Army, telling them that the city was weak and to attack now.'

Lord Taku frowned. 'The King's weakness has given Lord Chancellor Mzia great powers. He has always wanted to be ruler.' He traced the hook-shaped scar on his cheek with his finger.

'Can you not warn the King?' Oriole said. 'You were friends once – surely he would listen to you.'

'Ai . . .' Lord Taku sighed. 'We have not spoken to each other since the Fell. We are like strangers now.'

'What if I go to him?' she said. 'What if I tell him who I am?'

Lord Taku shook his head. 'The King is in very poor health. If you mention the Prince, it might bring back painful memories. Even though you are his granddaughter, I am afraid of what he might do.'

Lady Butterfly took the children aside. 'Come, I will show you both where you will be sleeping,' she said.

The house was built around an inner courtyard. There was a well in the centre where fresh water was drawn, and a small grove of fruit trees. There was also a vegetable garden. The floor of the courtyard was covered in round stepping stones edged with soft moss.

Lady Butterfly slid open a door that led off the courtyard, and there on the floor were two padded sleeping mats woven from fine reeds and covered with bright-green silk quilts. A low wooden table stood in the corner with two ceramic cups on it. Lady Butterfly filled the cups with a liquid that was the colour of tea and told them it would help them sleep. She pointed to a low stand.

'Over there is some water and a cloth for you to wash, Oriole.' Then she wrinkled her nose. 'Boy, come with me to the bathhouse. You need a good scrubbing.'

Boy didn't much like the sound of that, but with a reluctant smile at Oriole he followed Lady Butterfly.

Oriole undressed by the light of a candle. Her dress was wearing thin. The jade dagger that she kept at her waist lay on the quilt. She looked at it a moment, wondering if she should try again to see the truth in the stones. *No,* she thought. *I am too tired.*

Oriole soaked the cloth in the water and cleaned herself. How good it felt. She ran a hand over her shoulder, feeling her smooth skin. There was no sign of feathers or wings now. The thought that she could change into a bird gave her strength. And it also excited her. She longed to tell Mellow. *Had he known about this all along?* she wondered.

A pale blue nightgown with a single butterfly embroidered on the collar lay on one of the beds. She tried it on. It was a perfect fit.

On a table in the corner was a framed mirror edged

with inlays of mother of pearl. Oriole had only dreamt about mirrors through Mellow. She had never seen one in real life. She inspected her face and smiled and the reflection smiled back. Then, for some reason, she shivered and she did not know why. Here in Lord Taku's house, surely, they were safe. Touching the glass, she almost expected her hand to go through it and her fingers to touch warm skin on the other side.

When Boy returned from his bath, sweet-smelling and transformed, the children snuggled down into their beds and were soon fast asleep, oblivious to the danger that lurked nearby.

Outside the city, the Barbarian Army approached with confidence. They knew the city was theirs to seize whenever they wanted.

The King had taken to his bed, his face pale, his breathing shallow.

And in the Forest of Birds, Mellow, too, was waning.

The Forest grew dark as the birds huddled miserably in the branches of the ancient Banyan tree.

Someone has to find Oriole,' Redbill said.

And the birds all nodded. They knew he was right,

but no one dared venture into the city. So they sat and sighed and watched the Eastern skies, hoping for a message on the Wind.

22
THE DOMED ROOM

The following morning Lady Butterfly appeared at the door to the children's room.

'Come and eat,' she said to Oriole and Boy. She was wearing a coral-pink gown and tiny pink slippers with a butterfly tassel on the toes.

They dressed quickly. Both were hungry and felt refreshed. There were new clothes for Oriole hanging on a hook – a yellow tunic with long bell-shaped sleeves, and pants to match. And a beaded belt, which she used to secure the precious jade dagger at her waist. There were boots, too, but they were made of leather and the scent of animal was still strong on them. Oriole put her own worn shoes made from twisted vines back on.

Boy's clothes had been cleaned and were draped on a

stool by his bed. He wasn't sure if he liked his new clean self or the smell of soap on his skin. It made him sneeze and his nose itch. But Oriole gave him a big hug when he was dressed and called him her handsome Boy, which made him blush. Maybe his clean self was not too bad after all.

Lord Taku was already at the table eating breakfast when they came into the kitchen. There was millet porridge, nuts and pickled vegetables, baked flat bread filled with onions and spices, and sweet milk tea.

Boy made loud slurping noises while eating his porridge until Oriole nudged him under the table with her knee. She looked pointedly at Lord Taku. The old man was strangely quiet and Lady Butterfly kept looking at him.

After breakfast Lord Taku rose from the table. Lady Butterfly beckoned the children to follow.

'Where are we going?' Boy whispered to Oriole.

'I do not know,' Oriole replied. 'But I feel that he is leading us towards a thing that is very important.'

Lord Taku stopped on the verandah that bordered the inner courtyard. Beside him was a very small door low to the ground. Lady Butterfly bent down and slid the door open. She let her uncle go in first. He bent his back and stepped through.

Lady Butterfly delicately lifted her skirt and followed.

'Come in quickly,' she said. 'We must not let them get out.'

Boy looked at Oriole and they stepped inside.

There was a set of winding steps. As they neared the top step, a strange sound filled Boy's ears. Oriole gasped in recognition and leapt up the last few steps and through the door at the top.

Boy followed her and stopped, mouth gaping. They were standing in an immense room where a lush forest grew. It was like climbing into another world. Trees with feathery branches brushed the high domed ceiling, and flying in and out of the trees were hundreds of brightly coloured creatures.

Oriole laughed with tears in her eyes. 'Birds!' she cried. 'These are birds, Boy!'

A pair of purple birds with yellow heads landed on Lord Taku's shoulder. He gently shrugged them off and they flew away, chattering to each other. Other birds seemed shy, keeping to the top-most branches, peering down at them, heads cocked in curiosity.

Then a small blue bird with a smudge of white across its chest fluttered around Oriole. She put out her hand and it landed on her palm. She smiled and sang to it and it sang back to her.

Boy tried to entice a bird to sit on his arm.

'Keep still, Boy,' Oriole said. 'You are frightening them waving your arms around like that.'

Boy tried to keep still but was too excited at seeing these strange creatures, and so many of them.

'Lord Taku,' said Oriole, 'why are these birds here? I thought they were all killed or banished?'

'When the King had the forests cut down and the birds destroyed,' Lord Taku said. 'I collected as many as I could and brought them here.'

'So this is a secret place?' Boy said.

'Yes. And the secret must stay in this room.'

Boy turned to look at Oriole. She was not beside him. He looked around, then up to the tallest tree. Oriole was climbing through the branches. She was like a bird, hopping from one branch to another without hesitation. When she was almost at the top, she sat down. A bird with a long trailing tail sat on the branch beside her and began to chatter to her. Oriole replied in the same sing-song tone.

At once there was a hush as every bird fell silent. Then Oriole lifted her head and sang. It was a song about the forests that once filled the Kingdom of Pafir, about her mother, the bird girl Nightingale, and her handsome father, the Prince. It was about music and yearning and

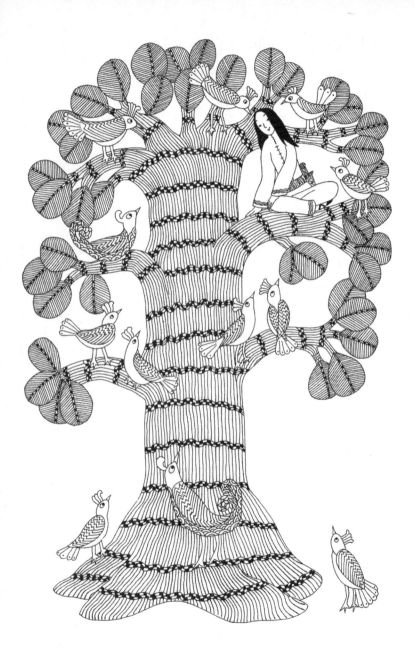

belonging. And about the dying King and his magical Wishbird, Mellow.

Lady Butterfly pulled a handkerchief from her sleeve and dabbed at her eyes. Even Lord Taku's eyes were moist with tears. Boy stood in awe, watching Oriole, his heart aching for his beautiful sad bird girl.

23

FLY AWAY, ORIOLE

As soon as Oriole finished her song, the birds began acting strangely. They called out to each other in alarm. They flew from branch to branch as if trying to escape from an invisible enemy.

'What is wrong with the little ones, Uncle?' Lady Butterfly said.

Oriole lifted her head. She heard heavy boots on hard ground and the clinking of metallic swords. She recognised the sound. And now she could smell the men, a rancid, sickening smell.

'Soldiers,' she called. 'They are outside.'

'Quickly, child, come down,' Lord Taku said.

But it was too late.

The King's soldiers, led by Lord Chancellor Mzia and

Panther, flooded into the Domed Room.

'There she is!' cried Panther, pointing up to where Oriole was perched.

Birds fluttered helplessly as the soldiers trampled through their forest. In their frenzy the small creatures flew into walls, falling to the ground stunned or dead.

'You are under arrest, Taku!' the Lord Chancellor shouted.

The guards bound Lord Taku's hands together. They did the same to Lady Butterfly and Boy.

'Cut down that tree! The girl won't escape this time.'

'You do not have to do that, Mzia,' Lord Taku said in desperation. 'I will coax her down. She will listen to me.'

'Too late for that, Taku. So this is where you've been hiding all this time. The King should have locked you away with the other musicians. I always despised him for bestowing favours upon you.' He waved his arm around him. 'This forest, and all these birds, that is a crime punishable by death. And now you are harbouring a runaway prisoner with the singing tongue,' he hissed.

'And you, Mzia, are a traitor. I know of your plan with Big Mo Ding to take over the Kingdom.'

'Whether you know it or not, it makes no difference,' Mzia laughed. 'The King is on his deathbed, the Kingdom of Pafir is as good as mine.' He turned to the tree where

Oriole sat high in the branches. 'Cut it down!'

Boy, Lord Taku and Lady Butterfly watched helplessly as the soldiers began hacking at the trunk with their axes. Oriole tried to climb higher, but there was nowhere to escape to.

Little hearts stopped beating and birds fell to the ground. Others were crushed as branches fell. The ones still alive were captured in a huge net.

From up on high, through a veil of tears, Oriole's anger grew. It twisted and burned inside her belly, making her skin itch as if a hundred mosquitoes were biting her. The turquoise feathers sprouted on her back and shoulders, more quickly this time. Her arms changed into wings and with the faith of a creature who has known flight all its life, Oriole leapt from the topmost branch.

She flew straight at the Lord Chancellor, who stood frozen in shock. She kicked him as hard as she could and the blow caught him on the chin. He staggered backwards.

The soldiers rushed at Oriole, cutting the air with their swords, missing her as she swooped and circled and landed on a branch to catch her breath. She charged at them again and again. It was as if a ball of fire was burning inside her and she blazed fury.

'Fools!' Mzia cried, wiping the blood from his chin. 'Chop down all the trees!'

The soldiers began hacking at the trunks and branches. As each tree crashed to the ground, Oriole flew to the next and the next until there were no more for her to land upon. But she did not give up. With her last burst of strength, she flew to the domed ceiling.

'She is tiring,' Lady Butterfly said, turning her face away in grief.

Boy couldn't bear to look and he too turned away. He caught sight of Panther in the corner, smirking at him.

As anger turned to despair, the feathers on Oriole's body disappeared and her wings finally became arms. She fell to the ground. The fire inside had died.

24
OLD ARDI

In the Forest of Birds there had been always the sound of the wind in the trees, the chirruping of insects underground and the clicking of beaks as the birds readied themselves for sleep. In her Forest Oriole never felt alone.

She woke from unconsciousness in the dungeon. Silence and darkness closed in around her. Her body ached and stung. She felt blood on her knees and bruises along one arm and a gash over her eyebrow.

She thought of Lord Taku, Lady Butterfly and Boy. *Had they been killed back there in the Domed Room? Or are they here in the dungeons too?*

'Boy?' she called softly. 'Boy . . . ?'

But there was only the echo of her own voice. She looked up at the window in the roof and thought back to that night when she saw Boy's small face peering down with the moon on his shoulder. Then another thought sent a spark of hope through her.

Old Ardi!

There was the sound of doors opening and closing, keys rattling, footsteps growing louder. She sat up hopefully. The door opened, its hinges straining against the wood. A shadow stood in the entrance.

Oriole's throat tightened. It was not Old Ardi. It was Lord Chancellor Mzia.

Mzia stepped into the dungeon, closing the door behind him.

If only I had the jade dagger, Oriole thought, *I would plunge it into your black heart.* She felt a tingling on her skin but breathed deeply. She did not want to change, not now, not for such a dark deed.

'I was the one who ordered your parents be killed,' he said in a voice as smooth as a pond covered with ice. 'The Prince and that . . . that creature you call a Mother.'

The words were like arrows shot straight into Oriole's heart. 'You?' she said, her voice trembling.

'They were in the way. Well, your father was. But then chance opened a door. I couldn't have planned it any better myself. Your father, the fool, rode off into the forest to hunt and there he met a bird girl and didn't want to return to the Palace. So to make certain he didn't change his mind, I had them both killed.' He pulled out an apple, wiped it on his sleeve and bit into it as if he had won a great victory. 'But then you came along and ruined all my plans. You as Princess are now the rightful heir to the throne and I cannot have this. Not when I've been plotting for so long and am so close to achieving my goal. When I join forces with Big Mo Ding we will conquer the surrounding kingdoms and I will be ruler of them all.' Mzia's eyes shone brightly.

Oriole turned away. She did not care for life any longer. When the King died, so too would her beloved Mellow. So she waited for death. But it did not come. Instead, she heard the door open.

'Why do you not kill me now?' she called.

'Because, my Princess, I cannot be seen as a murderer, can I? Too many men know you are here. But it will be done soon, you can be sure of that.'

Oriole's tears soaked the stone floor, her sadness seeped into the walls. She cried until there were no tears left inside.

'Oriole,' came a voice close to her ear. She felt a hand with rough skin lift up her head.

'It is Old Ardi.' The old guard was kneeling beside her. 'Listen, my child,' he said, helping her to sit up. 'I'm old and a little stupid, but a strange thing has happened to me since meeting you.' He smiled. 'Instead of losing my memories as old people do, mine have grown sharper. I remember how the City of Solace used to be before the Fell. I remember that people were once happy. Then the King lost his only son and it was as if a fog descended over everyone and they forgot to be kind . . . Old Ardi too. Then today I saw Lord Taku being brought down to the dungeons. I knew who he was straightaway as I've been here for many, many years. And he still remembered me. Lord Taku told me about you and where you have come from and why you are here. He said that it is written in a prophecy that in a time of great despair, a person of royal blood will deliver the Kingdom from its troubles. You must fulfil the prophecy, my Princess, and give memory and music and laughter back to us all.'

Oriole trembled against his warm, kind hands. 'How can I do this, Old Ardi? I am only a girl. I cannot make the King well, or stop the Barbarian Army from attacking. And I have lost the precious jade dagger, the only thing that might enable me to see the truth.'

'Maybe this will help . . .' Old Ardi placed the dagger in Oriole's hand.

Her eyes widened. 'How did you come by it?'

He smiled and patted her hand. 'I've worked here a

long time, child, and I have friends inside the Palace.'

The dagger felt heavy in Oriole's hand, different. A small flame re-kindled inside her.

Old Ardi smiled once more and left her, the door swinging open behind him.

25
TRUTH IN THE STONES

Oriole sat down on the floor of the dungeon holding the dagger on the palm of her hand. She ran her finger over the surface of the ruby and then the emerald. They were as bright as the eyes of a midnight owl.

At first Oriole did not know if she was imagining things. She wanted to see the truth in the stones so badly. But this time there seemed to be a movement – a flicker of light in the emerald. Not daring to blink, Oriole concentrated on the emerald, looking into its depths. And there she saw an image.

It was a picture of herself soaring over the lakes to the Forest of Birds. And in that moment Oriole knew the truth. The only way to cure Mellow and the King was for them to be together. She would bring Mellow back.

'But how will I fly if I can only grow wings when I am angered?' she asked the stones.

This time, the ruby replied. In its blood-red heart she saw a fire growing. She closed her eyes, imagining the fire inside her own heart, spreading through her body. She thought of Mellow and Boy and her heart swelled and the fire burned. Her skin began to itch and tingle. She did not need to be angry to make the change.

Now I know. The truth is not in the stones. It is inside me.

Oriole slipped the jade dagger into her belt. There was one thing she had to do before she left for the Forest.

Lord Taku lay in the corner of the cell with Lady Butterfly kneeling beside him. Boy rose to his feet when he saw Oriole. Then he ran to her and hugged her.

'The stones showed me the truth,' she said. 'I am returning to the Forest of Birds to bring Mellow back.'

'How are you going to fly all that way? You've only flown up to a roof and around the Domed Room . . .' Boy said.

'If the stones speak the truth, then it is what I must do,' she replied.

'Listen well, Oriole,' Lord Taku said. 'Outside this dungeon you will see an old watchtower that is no longer in use. Climb the stairs to the very top and leave from there. That way you will not be seen.'

Oriole nodded.

'And on your return, if the Barbarian Army has surrounded us, there is a secret tunnel, an escape route, that the royal family used in times of war. This tunnel passes from the Throne Room under the city walls to the outside.'

Oriole nodded gravely. 'How will I find the opening to the tunnel on my return?' she asked.

'You will see a large cluster of rocks in the shape of an eagle. Underneath that, you will find the entrance.'

'I will bring the Wishbird back, Lord Taku,' Oriole said.

But in her heart she knew that this was not enough. Mellow and the King might be cured of their illness when they were brought together, but the Barbarian Army was still on the attack. And nothing, it seemed, would stop them now.

26
FROM THE WATCHTOWER

Oriole climbed the steps of the watchtower, circling around and around until she reached the top. Drawing the jade dagger from her belt, she looked into the ruby, into the heart of it, and the fire held within. Immediately she felt the same fire in her own body, beginning in her chest where she felt the strong beat of her heart. Then it spread like cool water through her limbs.

Oriole's skin tingled. Feathers grew down her back and on her shoulders. Her arms changed into wings, sleek and beautiful.

Looking towards the west, towards the Forest, Oriole stepped off the watchtower and soared into the morning sky.

She flew high, higher than the birds who had brought

her to the City of Solace on their woven tapestry of leaves. So high that if you went outside and looked up, you would only see a tiny blue speck amongst the clouds. She flew through the day and into the night. Exhaustion pervaded every part of her body but she flew on, the fire in her heart burning more brightly than ever as she neared the Forest of Birds and her beloved Mellow.

Then she saw it, that lush expanse of green and, in the centre, towering majestically above the Forest, the ancient Banyan tree.

Oh, happy is my heart to see my home again, she thought. *The colours of green, the song of the birds, the cool shadows and sweet-smelling air.*

She landed on a branch of the old tree. It swayed gently beneath her. Oriole stepped into her nest and looked down. There lay a single gold feather from the crown on Mellow's head. She looked across at Fern Pond and a chill grew in her heart. *Am I too late? Has Mellow already . . .* She dared not say the word.

A darkness fell over her and her hearing dimmed. There was no more hope – the King, the City of Solace, the people, all finished.

There was a soft fluttering of wings and a chirping.

Oriole opened her eyes.

Redbill sat on a nearby branch. Then Purplewing

appeared and Yellowspot and Droplet. And finally the Peewee birds.

'Oriole has returned!' they cried.

'I have failed,' she said. 'I could not save our Mellow . . .'

'No, Oriole, there is still hope,' Redbill said. 'Hurry. He has been calling for you.'

'Mellow is still alive?' Oriole sprang to her feet and her wings fluttered around her.

The birds stared and stared. 'What has happened to you? Why, you have become a beautiful bird,' they said.

'I do not have time to explain, dear ones,' said Oriole. 'I must take Mellow to the City of Solace to be with his King. Where is he?'

'We moved him to Fire Rock where it is warm,' said Redbill.

Oriole beat her great wings in the air and flew away, leaving the birds staring after her in disbelief.

Mellow was lying on a soft bed of moss, his eyes half closed. He stirred when Oriole knelt down beside him.

'Dear, dear Mellow,' Oriole said, softly.

Mellow opened his eyes and saw a glorious bird girl with turquoise wings bending over him.

'Nightingale?' he whispered.

'No, it is Oriole,' she said. 'I have come to take you to your King.'

He smiled weakly and closed his eyes again.

'Droplet, Redbill, fetch my pouch from the Banyan tree so that I may carry Mellow safely inside it,' Oriole said.

Never before had the birds felt such reverence. Oriole had returned and she had changed. And it was not only her wings and feathers that were different. She had the aura of a Princess.

'Shall we come with you?' the birds asked when they returned with the pouch.

'Not this time,' Oriole replied as she gently placed Mellow inside it. She knew the way would be dangerous if the Barbarian Army was close. And after what had happened in the Domed Room . . .

'Goodbye, dear ones,' she said as she spread her wings.

'Safe journey, Princess,' they all cried.

The Wind was Oriole's friend. Sometimes it carried her on its back so that all she had to do was keep her wings outstretched. At other times it blew from behind so that she travelled at twice the speed. She knew the landmarks now and she knew when she was close. Mellow slept most of the way, warm inside the pouch.

As she drew close to the city walls, Oriole watched for the rock in the shape of an eagle. But she saw something else that made her tremble with fear.

A seething mass of soldiers surrounded the city.

27
A KING'S TEAR

Oriole found the opening to the tunnel covered with a metal grate. She pulled on the bars but they were held fast. She was trapped . . . on the outside. She thought of flying over the walls. That would be faster, and simpler . . . but also deadly, she realised. Even if the Barbarian soldiers did not shoot her down with their arrows, the guards on the walls would call out an alarm and she would be arrested as soon as she landed in the city. No, she had to use the tunnel.

The dagger! She suddenly remembered Lord Taku saying it was carved from jade so rare it could cut through metal.

She glanced at Mellow, lying still but safe in the pouch beside her, and set to work on one of the bars.

It snapped in her hand, rusty with age. It did not take long to cut through all the bars, and soon there was an opening large enough for Oriole to squeeze through with Mellow.

Inside the tunnel she found a basket of torches. She picked one up and lit it with a fire stick from a box nearby. The torch sizzled then burned brightly, lighting up a pathway under the city walls.

It seemed to take forever to reach a door, and when she saw it she rushed towards it eagerly. Carefully, she pushed it open, just a crack.

'We are almost there, Mellow,' she whispered, cradling him in the crook of her arm. Mellow had not stirred throughout the entire journey but now she felt him move. She looked down. 'Mellow?'

'My King is close. I feel him,' Mellow said. His eyes brightened.

'Oh, Mellow. You are growing well again.' Oriole kissed his golden crown and brought his soft cheek close to hers.

The opening to the Throne Room was covered by a large tapestry. She was about to draw it aside when she heard voices. She recognised the voice of Lord Chancellor Mzia.

'I have word that Big Mo Ding will attack at first light,'

the Lord Chancellor said. 'Order your soldiers to lay down their weapons, General. If we surrender, no one will be harmed.'

'It is my duty to protect the King and this city,' the General replied.

'The Kingdom of Pafir has already been conquered,' the Lord Chancellor scoffed. 'This city is the last stronghold. The King is close to death. We should surrender now.'

'What are you saying, Lord Chancellor?'

'That a new Kingdom will rise from the ashes, General, as will a new ruler. If you are willing to follow this ruler, he will make you his Lord Chancellor, I can promise you that.'

'I will die before serving that barbarian, Big Mo Ding.'

'It is not Big Mo Ding who will be ruler.'

There was a pause, then a shuffling of feet. 'You?' the General laughed. 'You want to be King?'

'Let us just say I know where our strengths lie and they cannot be served well under the present King,' Mzia said coolly.

'You are a traitor, Mzia!' the General shouted.

A moment later there was a mighty clash of steel. Oriole covered her ears with her hands, the sound was too terrifying. But she could still hear the grunts and groans, the cries of pain.

When at last there was silence, Mellow spoke. 'Oriole, it is over. Take me to the King, quickly.'

Oriole's heart beat wildly as she peered around the edge of the tapestry. Then she let out a small cry. There on the floor lay the General. His eyes stared lifelessly up at the ceiling.

'The General is dead. The Lord Chancellor has killed him,' she said with a shudder.

'Look away, child,' said Mellow. 'Take me to the King's chamber. It is across the Courtyard of Four Gingkoes. Hurry, now. But be careful. Mzia is more dangerous than ever now that blood is on his sword.'

Oriole ran down the hall and out into the courtyard.

'There,' Mellow said. 'It is the one with the gold carving on the door.'

The King lay on a large carved bed with a red silk canopy. A breeze lifted the cloth that hung down, making it billow like the sails of a ship.

The King stirred as Oriole approached. 'Who is there?' he asked weakly.

Oriole did not reply but set Mellow down on the yellow covers and stepped back into the shadows.

The King lifted his head from the pillow and stared blindly. 'Who is it? I cannot see you?'

Mellow walked across the bedcovers towards him. 'It is I, your Wishbird, my King,' he said. 'I have returned.'

The King reached out a hand to touch Mellow's golden crown. Then he stroked the Wishbird's chest with his finger, the way he used to do when he was a young boy. 'Mellow . . . It is you . . . I thought I was dreaming.' He pushed himself up in his bed and leaned towards Mellow, smiling tenderly. He lifted the Wishbird onto his lap. Mellow ruffled his feathers and let them fall back into place under the King's touch.

Oriole clasped her hands together as waves of joy came over her. A healthy pink flush was coming back to the King's face and Mellow's feathers were growing ever-brighter as she watched.

'My King,' Mellow said. 'There is someone I would like you to meet.' He flew to sit on Oriole's shoulder. 'This is your granddaughter, daughter of the Prince and his beloved, Nightingale.'

The King stared as Oriole stepped from the shadows. 'She is the girl . . . the one with the singing tongue . . .'

'Yes, my King, and her name is Oriole.'

The King rubbed his temples. 'I do not understand, Mellow.'

'Oriole has lived with me in the Forest of Birds since she was a baby. It was the request of your son and Nightingale, Oriole's mother, that I take her and protect her and raise her. And that is what I have done these past twelve years since I fled the Palace. Then I became ill and I knew something was wrong in the City of Solace. Oriole made this dangerous journey in order to make me – make us – well again.'

'I murdered my own son, Mellow,' the King said, sinking back into his pillows.

'No. They were murdered by Lord Chancellor Mzia,' said Oriole. 'And he has killed the General. He wants to take over your throne.'

The King looked at Oriole and then at Mellow.

'Is this true, Mellow?'

'I am afraid it is, my King. And now Big Mo Ding's army is poised to take the city at dawn.'

The King's eyes were wet with tears as he looked at Oriole. His chest heaved. Oriole went to the bed and sat down beside her grandfather. She placed her small hand in his.

'You are my flesh and blood, my son's own child,' he said gently, looking into her green eyes.

'Yes, Grandfather,' Oriole replied. 'And we must make this city live again.'

28
THE ATTACK

Big Mo Ding did not wait for morning before attacking. It was as if a monster had been unleashed, ripping with its tremendous claws at the city walls. The four gates of the city were being rammed.

Boom Boom Boooom.

The noise shook the ground. Troops of archers scrambled up onto the parapets and fired down at the enemy soldiers.

Frightened people ran onto the streets, their faces pale with terror. Some had packed their belongings in two bundles that they carried on each end of a bamboo pole across their shoulders. Others called their children inside and quickly shut their doors and windows. But there was nowhere to hide and nowhere to flee to.

Inside the Palace, Oriole sat with Boy. Lord Taku and Lady Butterfly were talking with the King. They spoke bravely, but there was a feeling of hopelessness in the air. Only Oriole seemed strong and sure.

'Why don't you flee, Oriole,' Boy said. 'Take Mellow and leave the city. Go back to your Forest.'

'Have you forgotten the prophecy that a person of royal blood will save the city?' Oriole said.

'We are surrounded, Oriole. Everyone will die when they break down the gates.'

As darkness fell, the Barbarian Army withdrew and camped outside the city. Tomorrow they would attack again and tomorrow they would take the City of Soulless.

Buildings were burning from the fireballs catapulted over the wall. The wounded were taken inside. Women and children cried and exhausted men sat dazed among the debris of the ruined city.

After the noise of battle the silence was eerie.

Oriole and Boy sat looking out of the Palace window at the smoke-filled sky. Mellow sat beside them, his head tucked under his wing.

'Life in the Forest of Birds is so simple,' Oriole sighed.

'The sun rises, the birds sing, the Wind sighs and the leaves dance. And in the centre of everything lives the ancient Banyan tree, master of all.'

It was at that very moment, when she was thinking about her beloved Banyan tree, that a seedling thought sprouted in her mind. Oriole sat very still for a moment. Then she jumped up and said, 'Thank you, thank you!'

'What is the matter, child?' Mellow said.

'The ancient Banyan tree sent me a dream,' Oriole replied.

Mellow sat back to listen.

'Music has the power to change the hearts of humans, is that not so?' began Oriole.

'Yes, and you can see what has happened here. Without music the city has died,' replied Mellow.

Oriole sat down, then stood up again. The dream had excited her. 'Well, the soldiers on the other side of the wall are humans, too. They have hearts just like you and me so they must cry and love and long for things. And it is at night when all is quiet that they must think about home. I will sing to them, Mellow. I will sing the most beautiful song they have ever heard.'

Mellow nodded and the feathery crown on the top of his head waved as if in slow motion. 'It is worth a try,' he said. 'It is certainly worth a try.'

Boy didn't know how music could change the hearts of men who had been trained to kill. But he didn't say so to Oriole.

It was just after midnight and the moon hid behind streaky grey clouds as if it were too scared to look down upon the scene below.

Outside the city walls all was quiet. The enemy soldiers huddled around their campfires. Tomorrow they would fight and conquer.

Oriole stood at the top of the old watchtower. She looked out at the spots of flickering flames that could just as easily have been orange butterflies on a warm summer's night instead of men with weapons ready to kill. For a brief second she wondered if her plan could really work. Had she been naive in thinking that music could change the hearts of men?

She shook her doubts aside. Mellow had told her that music came from the soul of the earth and that is why it spoke to everyone. She had to believe this was true.

The best songs came to Oriole on the wings of dreams – the tune and the words appearing in her head as if sent down from the stars. But the air felt too tight and smelled too much of metal, fire and pitch. Around the top of the tower were four large windows. Oriole stood at the one facing west, facing towards her home in the Forest of Birds. She looked up at the stars and took a deep breath in.

But there were no words on her lips, no music in her head. It was as if a weight, a darkness, pressed down on the lightness of song within her.

Oriole turned at the sound of a creak on the staircase.

'Who is there,' she called, thinking it might be Boy even though she had told him to stay in the Palace. She needed to be alone for this, the most important moment of her life.

When there was no answer she tiptoed to the railing and peered over the edge. The staircase spiralled downwards into blackness and Oriole felt a warning chill.

Unsheathing the jade dagger at her belt, she stepped back into the shadows and waited.

A rat came up the steps and scurried across the floorboards. She turned to watch it and breathed out in relief. 'You frightened me, little friend. Next time —'

An arm came around Oriole's neck.

'I should have killed you when I first saw you,' Lord Chancellor Mzia said in her ear. Oriole smelt blood and death. 'But now, little bird, it is time to fly.'

Oriole tried turning and stabbing wildly behind her, but her blows did not make contact.

Mzia twisted her arm painfully and the dagger clattered to the floor. Then he began dragging Oriole towards the window. His arm was so tight about her throat that ghostly shapes danced before her eyes and she fought to stay conscious. *I must sing,* she willed. But Mzia's arm was cutting off her voice. And then her air.

The last thing Oriole saw was the City of Solace burning.

29
DEATH WISH

Suddenly Mzia cried out in pain and loosened his grip on Oriole's throat. The light returned to her eyes. She took in big gulps of air. Mzia was turning his head, grabbing at something on his back, whirling around like a mad man. He fell against the wall and slid to the floor.

It was then that Oriole saw Boy with the dagger in his hand. He had stabbed Mzia in his side.

Oriole let out a great sigh of relief that turned into a yelp of terror as Mzia rose from the floor and lunged at them. 'Boy, behind you!' she cried.

Boy turned and slashed with the dagger, but Mzia grabbed Boy's hand and lifted him off the ground, preparing to fling him out of the window. Boy kicked and fought but he was helpless.

In desperation, Oriole opened her mouth and began to sing. The music poured from her and coiled around Mzia like a rope of metal spikes. It tore through him, twisting and wrapping and squeezing his black heart. He let go of Boy and staggered backwards trying to rid himself of the pain. A scream echoed around the tower as he fell through the window.

Oriole and Boy crawled over to the edge of the tower, shaking. Far below them lay the Lord Chancellor's crumpled body.

With Boy's support, Oriole staggered to the western corner of the tower and looked out.

It was time to save the City of Solace.

The song that Oriole could not summon before came in a wave, surging up from the earth and shimmering down from the stars.

The King, who was sitting in the Throne Room, lifted his head. His mouth opened slightly and his breathing calmed. Never before had he heard anything more sublime. The haunting notes spoke to him, reminding him of the pain he had caused his people and his son. He reached out his hand as if Oriole was standing before him. How he loved this strange and beautiful child.

Mellow flew to the King's side. His eyes shone and his feathers once more gleamed.

'She will save the Kingdom, my King.'

'I think she will, Mellow,' the King replied.

Oriole's song touched the ears of the soldiers on the other side of the wall. It told them of grassy plains stretching to the foot of snow-covered peaks, of a woman waiting for her husband, of children waiting for their father, of a dog waiting for its master. It was a sad song, a hollow wind song. But it also told of happiness. New grass shoots through melting snow. A family sitting by a warm fire in their home made of animal skins, waiting. While camels and horses graze outside, a dog keeps watch, always alert, always looking towards the south. The Wind brings the smell of battle to its nostrils. It raises its shaggy head as it scents its master. With excited yelps the dog runs out to meet the weary soldier. The wife and children lift the flap of their tent. He has come home at last.

The soldiers, huddled around campfires and lying wet and cold on the frosty ground, listened in rapt silence. As Oriole's song carried over the city walls, souls were stirred and hearts began to yearn for the families they had left behind. Why had they come to fight in a strange and distant land? What had this war to do with them?

They began to mutter and murmur restlessly. Only Big Mo Ding, whose heart was black as coal dust, heard nothing. He threw off the fur that he lay under and stood

up, wondering what had come over his men. He looked towards the watchtower and then he shouted, 'It's a trick! Pick up your weapons. We attack now!'

But the soldiers did not move.

Inside the City of Soulless, the townspeople stepped out of their houses. They, too, listened in wonder. They remembered – yes, they remembered – how it was before the Fell, before the world turned grey. And they remembered how they used to laugh and dance and sing.

Oriole's music gave every listener a dream. Boy's dream was of the garden of his long-ago home. Of his ana and ata making music as birds flew in and out of the trees. As he stood beside Oriole, he felt a strange thrumming almost like music under his feet, as if the walls themselves were trying to speak.

When Oriole sang out the last note, she had to hold onto the window ledge. The song had taken all of her strength. The walls began to spin and in an instant, as she collapsed, Boy was at her side.

30
GOLDEN NOTES

In a corner of the Palace courtyard, under the shade of one of the gingko trees, two musicians began to play. The man played a three-string violin and the woman a zither. Their eyes were closed and their bodies swayed together. It was an old song, one they had not played in ten or so years. But once it had been the most popular song in the City of Solace.

The golden notes floated across the courtyard, finding their way to Boy who was sleeping on a mat in the Throne Room. He was dreaming of his mother's soft skin, a swinging jade earring, a flash of peach-pink silk and a long royal-blue robe.

He opened his eyes. Then he remembered last night and he sat up.

'Oriole!' he cried. He had carried her down from the watchtower, step by endless step, before collapsing at the bottom.

'You are awake,' Lord Taku said as he and Lady Butterfly entered the room.

'Where is Oriole, Lord Taku? Is she all right?' Boy asked.

Lord Taku smiled. 'She is in the Courtyard of Four Gingkoes. Come ... I want to show you something.'

Boy rose from his mat and followed Lord Taku to the window.

'If you look down there,' Lord Taku said, 'you will see her. And you will also see two other people you might remember.'

Boy looked down into the courtyard. Oriole was sitting on a rock in front of two musicians.

'They are your ana and ata, Boy,' Lady Butterfly said, softly. 'Why don't you go down and join them.'

Boy held onto the wall, barely able to speak. 'But where ... where have they been all this time?'

'The King locked up all the musicians within the city walls,' Lord Taku said, his hand on Boy's shoulder.

'We called them the crying walls ... we thought it was the wind,' Boy said, softly.

'Go to them, child. They have been waiting to see

you for a very long time.'

'And the city, Lord Taku? Did we save the city?'

Lord Taku nodded and pointed beyond the city walls. The camp was empty, only the fires were left smoking. The Barbarian Army had gone.

Boy ran down the steps of the Palace, along the corridor and out into the bright sunshiny courtyard. Then he stopped, shy all of a sudden, breathless.

Oriole came to him and squeezed his hand.

Boy's mother had her hair tied back off her neck with red thread. She was thin and very pale but her fingers were nimble, gliding over the strings of the zither like water slipping over rocks. Boy's father played a violin. His hair was grey and he had a small beard. His body swayed as he moved the bow.

Boy looked at Oriole and she smiled back and nodded.

As the last notes lingered in the air and then melted away, Boy's ana and ata looked up and saw him. Their eyes glowed with love.

'My name is Boy,' Boy said, his voice small.

'Hero,' his mother whispered, her eyes dancing like sun on the water. 'Your true name is Hero.'

'Come, Hero,' Ata said, and he patted the space beside him.

Boy sat between his mother and father.

Ata placed the violin in Boy's hand. 'We will teach you to play music, Hero. Would you like that?'

Boy felt the instrument in his hand and it felt right, it felt good. 'Yes, I would like that,' he said, his face shining.

Then they drew him in close. Their heads touched, images whirled, spun, flew. For the moment there was no need for words.

31
THE BIRDS WILL RETURN

Oriole walked into the Throne Room and found Mellow sitting on the windowsill, preening himself.

'Where are Lord Taku and Lady Butterfly?' she asked.

'They have returned home to free the birds,' Mellow replied.

Oriole looked out the window. 'When are we going home, Mellow?'

'You forget, child, that I am the King's Wishbird. I cannot go back to the Forest of Birds. Now that the King is well it is my duty to stay here. I belong here.'

Oriole's heart gave a lurch. She never thought that she would have to return to the Forest of Birds without her beloved Mellow.

'Oh, but I thought . . . yes, of course,' she said, hiding

her disappointment. 'And Grandfather? I would like to say goodbye to him before I go.'

'He is in the Chamber of Celestial Notes,' Mellow said, watching her intently. 'Go down to the Hall of Virtue, turn left into the Waterfall Room. It is the eighth door on your right.' Then he turned back to look at the city.

Oriole followed Mellow's directions with a heavy heart. She had not realised how big the Palace was. She had only seen a quarter of it and she had never been in this part before. It was dark and dusty and had obviously been shut off for years.

She counted the doors . . . four, five, six, seven . . .

When she reached the eighth door, she found it ajar. She quietly pushed it open.

The windows were folded back and sunlight splashed across the floor. The King stood at a carved table, his back to Oriole, unaware that she was there. The tabletop was bare except for a long thin box, which sat in the centre. The King touched the lid, running his finger lovingly over it. Then he lifted the corner of his robe and began to wipe off years of dust. The wood underneath was so beautiful it gleamed and Oriole could see the King's reflection in its surface. His face was sad and wistful.

With two hands he carefully lifted out a wooden instrument.

The King brought the flute to his lips and began to play. Oriole's body tingled. The sound was like that of a bird, with notes so sweet that tears welled in her eyes. It gave her a dream of her Forest home. And her heart ached for her friends, for her nest in the ancient Banyan tree, for Fern Pond and Fire Rock.

The notes lingered long after the King had finished.

There was a silence, then Oriole said, 'That was beautiful, Grandfather.'

'Music reflects what is in one's heart,' the King replied, turning to face her.

'Yes,' she said. 'Grandfather, my heart tells me that I must go back to the Forest of Birds even though Mellow will stay here with you.'

'This is your home now, Oriole. You belong here in the Palace. When I pass on, this Kingdom will be yours to rule with Mellow at your side.'

Oriole sighed. 'I have seen so many things here that make me sad and I cannot make myself unsad about them. Only the Forest of Birds can do that.'

'Together we can change these sad things, Oriole,' the King said. 'There are many people here who love you – Lord Taku, Lady Butterfly, Hero, Mellow, and of course me, your old grandfather.' He smiled. 'In the Forest all you have are trees and birds and insects. Even your mother wanted human company in the end.'

'Mother and Father chose to stay in the Forest too, Grandfather,' she reminded him. She put her hand in his. 'I will miss you all, but I will visit, often . . .'

'I beg you to stay. You are my only family. We will replant the forests and the birds will return and so will the music. The City of Solace will live again.'

'I know you will do that, Grandfather. Mellow will help you. He will mend the broken threads of the world as he has always done.' She squeezed his hand. 'I am tired. I will sleep now. But I will leave tomorrow.'

That night Oriole left the window of her bedroom wide open so that she could gaze out at the moon as she always did from her nest in the ancient Banyan tree.

She heard a fluttering and something flew through the window and landed on the bed beside her.

'Listen, Oriole, and do not speak,' Mellow said.

Oriole sat up, hugging her knees to her chest.

'You belong here with your grandfather. It is not only he who needs you, the entire Kingdom of Pafir does too. The Forest of Birds will always be there, just as it has been since the first seed of the Banyan tree blew from across the

Kun Lun Mountains and burrowed into the ground. You have come home now, Oriole. Home is here. And here is where you belong, where you are loved, where you will one day be a great and gracious Queen.'

'But what if I do not want all that, Mellow? How can I live in a Palace with walls, in a city with walls, with so many humans who make noise, when all I have known is the Forest and green and quiet?'

'What about Hero? Will he not grieve for you?'

'He has his ana and ata now. He has a home where he belongs,' Oriole said. 'I belong in the Forest climbing trees and eating roots and berries, like I have always done.'

'I will not stop you from leaving, Oriole, for you are now grown and are strong and wise. But think carefully before you choose to go.'

'Thank you. I will, Mellow,' she said, and she stroked his golden crown of feathers.

When Mellow left to return to the King's chamber, Oriole lay down. She drew her coat of rainbow feathers around her and thought about her nest in the arms of the ancient Banyan tree. *It will need repairing. And it will be full of leaves.* She smiled. The pull of the Forest was strong, like the moon pulling the tides. But Mellow would not be with her. Would the Forest of Birds be the same without him? And Hero would not be there. Hero, whom she loved almost as much as Mellow.

But I can visit the city whenever I please. I can fly now. If the Wind is kind it will only take me a day.

She turned and lay on her side. Her hand touched the silver box that held the turquoise blue feather, her mother's feather.

She snapped open the box and held the feather up by its quill. A hush fell over the room.

Perhaps Mellow is right, she thought. *Perhaps my place is here in the Palace with Grandfather and the people I love. I could make the City of Solace beautiful, as beautiful as a forest even. I would plant trees in every empty space and the birds would return. Yes, the birds would return just as the music and the laughter has.*

A smile, only a small one at first, grew on Oriole's face. She lifted her eyes to the window, to the open space of the midnight sky.

And there in the distance, on the old city wall, a nightingale sang to the moon.

EPILOGUE

Come, take a stroll with me down the Palace Road and through the market place, for I want to show you something. It is busy today with camels and carts and sweet brown-eyed donkeys. It is market day. People from the Borderlands are setting up their stalls. Tarpaulins of every colour are strung between bamboo poles. Laid out on the ground beneath them are exotic rugs, silver and bead jewellery, jars and vases and pots in all manner of shapes, colours and sizes. There are instruments from all over the Kingdom of Pafir – violins, flutes, zithers and trumpets. For music can be heard now down lanes and alleyways, from doorways, from windows, and even from rooftops.

Now we are passing Lord Taku's walled garden.

See there . . . a gate has been built and children are playing hide-and-seek in the trees.

There is Lady Butterfly sitting with Hero at a small food cart by the wall. Rabbit is chatting and rolling dough, making his special chilli noodle broth. He has become quite famous now in the City of Solace. He waves at us, inviting us over for a snack, but we do not have time to stop.

Are you looking around for Panther? You won't find him hanging around here. He has disappeared, and nobody has seen him since his betrayal.

We are leaving now through the Western Gate. It is not very far, the thing I want to show you. Just over the other side of those flat rocks. Tread carefully and watch your step, for the thing I want to show you is still so young and precious and fragile.

Here we are. Bend down and look closely. There, can you see it?

See that tiny brave tree pushing up through the dry cracked earth? That is the first tree of a mighty forest that will one day grow lush around the City of Solace. And do you know where it came from? It is a seed from the ancient Banyan tree, borne here by the Wind. It sprouted on the dawn of that day, the day when I first sang the Song of the Wishbird.

ACKNOWLEDGEMENTS

So often an author sits alone, eyes gazing inwards, writing about the pictures she sees on the wall of her imagination. Yet at the same time there are many who help along the way, from the book's conception to its birth. And these are the people I would like to thank.

The idea for *The Wishbird* goes way back – to a time before I was born. The year is 1935. My mother is twelve years old. One day she finds a book tucked away in a cupboard in her classroom at Rathdowne Street Primary School in Melbourne. The book is called *Green Mansions*. It is written for adults but the story so captivates her that it awakens a life-long love of books.

As an adult my mother scoured Melbourne for a copy of *Green Mansions*. Only after years of searching did she finally find it in a second-hand bookshop.

I was fourteen when she first gave *Green Mansions* to me to read. The story about a forest-dwelling girl called Rima has haunted me ever since. I did not know, then, that I would be a writer and that one day this book would be the seed for one of my own books. But what a strange and wondrous thing life is. Something that you think is unimportant can grow into a mighty forest.

And so the first person I would like to thank is the teacher who, more than eighty years ago, left *Green Mansions* in the classroom cupboard for my mother to discover.

Thank you also to those at Penguin: my friend and publisher, Jane Godwin, and my editor Katrina Lehman and book designer Tony Palmer for their faith and patience and understanding.

To my daughter, Lei Lei, who spent many hours with me editing the early drafts in her New York apartment.

To my son, Ren, who read and edited and made so many valuable suggestions.

To my dog, Hero, who lent his name to my main character and keeps me sane while I'm working.

To my wonderful husband, Steve, my first editor and ideas man of knowledge, the one who is always there to give me encouragement and inspiration when I need it.

To Varuna, the writers' house in the Blue Mountains, and their Fellowship retreat which allowed me the space to write and illustrate in such a serene and beautiful setting.

Lastly, thank you to my mum who read and edited the manuscript and for being that inquisitive little girl in the classroom.

ABOUT THE AUTHOR

Gabrielle Wang is an award-winning author and illustrator born in Melbourne of Chinese heritage. Her maternal great grand-father came to Victoria during the Gold Rush and her father from Shanghai.

Gabrielle's first novel, *The Garden of Empress Cassia,* won the 2002 Aurealis Award, was shortlisted for the Queensland Premier's Literary Awards and was a CBCA Notable Book. *The Pearl of Tiger Bay* was shortlisted for the 2004 Aurealis Award and *The Lion Drummer* was a Notable Book in the 2009 CBCA Book of the Year Awards. *A Ghost in My Suitcase* won the 2009 Aurealis Award, was a CBCA Notable Book, was shortlisted for the 2011 Sakura Medal, and received a Highly Commended in the 2010 Prime Minister's Literary Awards.

Gabrielle's first young adult novel, *Little Paradise*, received a Highly Commended in the 2011 Prime Minister's Awards. Gabrielle's picture book *The Race for the Chinese Zodiac* was a Notable Book in the 2011 CBCA Awards and was shortlisted for the 2011 YABBA and WAYBRA Awards. She has also written four books in Penguin's best-selling Our Australian Girl series.

Gabrielle is an ambassador for the Victorian Premier's Reading Challenge.

The Wishbird is Gabrielle's latest book for children.

www.gabriellewang.com

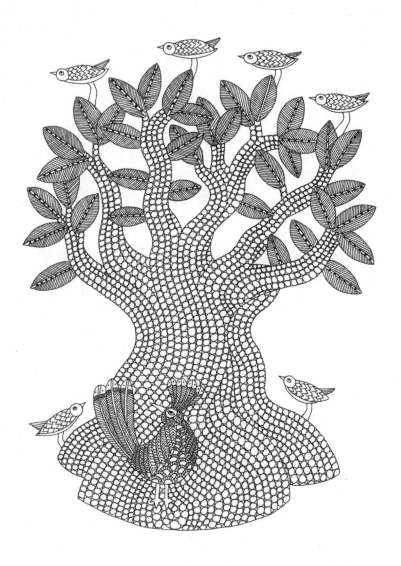